D0546631

PUFFIN CANADA

THE BELONGING PLACE

JEAN LITTLE is the award-winning author of forty-four books for children. Her picture books include *Once upon a Golden Apple* and *Revenge of the Small Small*. Her novel *Willow and Twig* won the Mr. Christie Book Award, *His Banner over Me* won the 1996 Violet Downey Book Award, and *Gruntle Piggle Takes Off* was nominated for a Governor General's Award for illustration. Her work has been translated into eighteen languages. She lives in Guelph, Ontario.

ЯTƧ

Also by Jean Little

FICTION

Willow and Twig

What Will the Robin Do Then?

His Banner Over Me

Different Dragons

Lost and Found

Spring Begins in March

Mama's Going to Buy You a Mockingbird

Stand in the Wind

One to Grow On

Mine for Keeps

Somebody Else's Summer

NON-FICTION

Little by Little

Stars Come Out Within

The Belonging Place

JEAN LITTLE

PUFFIN
CANADA

PUFFIN CANADA

Published by the Penguin Group

Penguin Group (Canada), 90 Eglinton Avenue East, Suite 700, Toronto, Ontario, Canada M4P 2Y3
(a division of Pearson Canada Inc.)

Penguin Group (USA) Inc., 375 Hudson Street, New York, New York 10014, U.S.A.
Penguin Books Ltd, 80 Strand, London WC2R 0RL, England
Penguin Ireland, 25 St Stephen's Green, Dublin 2, Ireland (a division of Penguin Books Ltd)
Penguin Group (Australia), 250 Camberwell Road, Camberwell, Victoria 3124, Australia
(a division of Pearson Australia Group Pty Ltd)
Penguin Books India Pvt Ltd, 11 Community Centre, Panchsheel Park, New Delhi – 110 017, India
Penguin Group (NZ), 67 Apollo Drive, Rosedale, North Shore 0632, New Zealand
(a division of Pearson New Zealand Ltd)
Penguin Books (South Africa) (Pty) Ltd, 24 Sturdee Avenue, Rosebank, Johannesburg 2196,
South Africa

Penguin Books Ltd, Registered Offices: 80 Strand, London WC2R 0RL, England

First published in a Viking Canada hardcover by Penguin Group (Canada),
a division of Pearson Canada Inc., 1997
Published in Puffin Canada paperback by Penguin Group (Canada),
a division of Pearson Canada Inc., 1998
Published in this edition, 2008

1 2 3 4 5 6 7 8 9 10 (WEB)

Copyright © Jean Little, 1997

All rights reserved. Without limiting the rights under copyright reserved above, no part of this
publication may be reproduced, stored in or introduced into a retrieval system, or transmitted in
any form or by any means (electronic, mechanical, photocopying, recording or otherwise), without
the prior written permission of both the copyright owner and the above publisher of this book.

Publisher's note: This book is a work of fiction. Names, characters, places and incidents
either are the product of the author's imagination or are used fictitiously, and any
resemblance to actual persons living or dead, events, or locales is entirely coincidental.

Manufactured in Canada.

LIBRARY AND ARCHIVES CANADA CATALOGUING IN PUBLICATION

Little, Jean, 1932–
The belonging place / Jean Little.

Originally published: Toronto : Viking, 1997.
ISBN 978-0-14-316741-9

I. Title.

PS8523.I77B45 2008   jC813'.54   C2007-906122-2ISBN-13: 978-0-14-316741-9

ISBN-13: 978-0-14-316741-9
ISBN-10: 0-14-316741-3

Except in the United States of America, this book is sold subject to the condition that it shall not, by
way of trade or otherwise, be lent, re-sold, hired out, or otherwise circulated without the publisher's
prior consent in any form of binding or cover other than that in which it is published and without
a similar condition including this condition being imposed on the subsequent purchaser.

Visit the Penguin Group (Canada) website at **www.penguin.ca**

Special and corporate bulk purchase rates available; please see
www.penguin.ca/corporatesales or call 1-800-810-3104, ext. 477 or 474

This one is for Jeanie and Ben and all kids who live with adoptive parents, grandparents, foster parents or others who love them so much that they share with them a belonging place.

Contents

Prelude

How I Got Started Writing My Book

*T*his story will really begin in the next chapter. So, if you hate reading prologues, you can skip this one. Six years after it ends, I fell off the haywagon and broke my leg. If I had not fallen, I would not be writing this. Don't blame me for parts you dislike; blame my brother Charlie. He pushed me.

"I barely touched her," he was insisting when I hit the ground with my right leg doubled up under me.

Yet, when I looked up, Charlie was staring down at me and his face was the picture of guilt. I tried to yell at him and found I was too winded even to whisper. I tried to move and it hurt far too much. More than I longed to tattle, I yearned for Mother to be there, holding me, making everything all right again.

Father did not realize anything was amiss at first. The noises made by Star's huge hooves and the creaking wagon wheels covered the sound of me tumbling off. Charlie should have said something but he was struck dumb. The wagon rolled on to where Hamish, the eldest of us, was waiting to pitch up the next stook. He had his back to me and, until he turned a minute later, did not notice that I was no longer perched beside Charlie on top of the load of hay.

My younger brother Hugh had just come back from the new house with a jug of cold tea for the workers. Sitting on the fence rail, he saw it all. He is eleven years of age but he can still be as brainless as a baby. He leaped down and shot off lickety-split, back to the house. I heard him shrieking, "Mother, come quick. Elspet's killed herself!"

Poor Mother! She was white as milk when she reached the hayfield. She dropped to her knees beside me without even glancing down first to make sure she would not land on a cow pat or a thistle. Her eyes were wide and dark with alarm and she was gulping for air.

"Oh, Elspet," she gasped, relief flooding her face, "thank the Lord you're alive. Are you badly hurt? Wait till I get my hands on Hugh for scaring me so!"

Her tender look told me again that she cared about me as much as she cared for the four children to whom she had given birth. But I have not doubted her love for me since I was nine. I would not have questioned it then if Jeanie Mackay's mother had not confused me by calling their wee Jamie "a changeling."

But I am jumping too far ahead.

Hamish, seeing Hugh's race to tell, turned, spotted me on the ground and came pelting across the stubble, and Father, seeing Hamish drop his pitchfork, jumped down and ran too, kneeling beside Mother, his eyes searching my face. He, too, was white under the weathered brown of his skin.

"I'm all right," I told them quickly. "I fell off the haywagon and my leg hurts, but I'm fine."

Then I started to shiver. Hearing my teeth chattering, Mother sent Charlie for Father's coat, which was hanging on a nearby fence post. As she tucked it snugly beneath my chin, I realized tears were spilling down my face.

"It's just the shock," Mother said, mopping up the flood. "Do not move or try to stand. I've sent Hamish off to Fergus to fetch the doctor. When Granny gets here, we'll see what we can do ourselves. Hold fast to that famous gumption of yours, my honey." Granny Ross had at last come from Scotland to join us in Canada. She had lived with us before we emigrated and, in the strange new land, we missed her sorely. Mother had miscarried twice during those first five years and, the minute she guessed another child was on the way, she begged Granny to come. Mother was no longer young and the hard life of a pioneer woman had taken its toll. Babies Granny brought into the world almost always throve.

Granny arrived on the next ship out and Hannah Ruth arrived on time for Christmas. She was small but lively and, with our prayers and Granny's careful tending, she will be two in December. Other children have contracted dread diseases but, so far, Ruth has stayed strong and well. God grant she continues to be what Granny calls "tough as a boot."

I had helped keep Ruth out from underfoot but, if my leg was really broken, I knew I would be helpless for weeks. As I thought of Ruth, tears began to flow again.

Granny put a stop to all such thoughts. She got to the field out of breath and gave me a sharp look which told me that she, too, had been worried. Then, before beginning to look at my hurts, she snapped, "Cease blubbing and give thanks to your Maker that you are all in one piece, lass. The hay won't be helped by a saltwater deluge."

I smiled as she intended me to. Then she began looking at my injury. When she was done, she declared it was a clean break and nothing to get in a pother about.

"Dinna stand gawping, William Gordon," she snapped at Father. "Lend a hand. I mun have some straight sticks."

She and Father made two strong splints to hold my leg stiff. When they were straightening it, making ready, I thought I would swoon from the pain, and Charlie, who had had the decency to stay, turned green. Granny bound the splints tightly with strips of stout cloth she had brought from the house, guessing how it would be. Then they shifted me gently onto a homemade stretcher and lifted me back onto the haywagon. I had not realized how it jolted until

Father started Star up the hill. Mother held my hand tightly, which kept me from crying out.

When we at last reached our new stone house, I was borne to the couch in the birthing room. I was so glad to be there that I never stopped to think that I would have to stay there, flat on my back, for weeks. Still, if the accident had happened a few months earlier, I'd have been lying on my back in our old log shanty, with only dim light and no privacy.

Hamish came back with the doctor at suppertime.

"If everyone were as handy as you, Mrs. Ross, I'd lose half my patients," the doctor joked, after inspecting my splints. "I'll leave it just as it is."

He gave me a bitter dose to dull the pain but, despite his draught, not only my injured leg but my entire body throbbed all night long.

I continued to hurt all over and did not feel like stirring hand or foot at first. I drifted in and out of sleep and, whenever I roused, Mother or Granny spooned broth or calves' foot jelly into me. Despite my bruises and the pain in my leg, I relished having the whole family cosseting me. Ruth was forever toddling in and patting me in a worried manner, which made me smile in spite of myself.

Then the doctor came again.

"Enough of this idling, young woman," he said. "You can be propped up now and take your turn at shelling peas or peeling apples. But you must on no account place any weight on that leg for another month at least, Elspet. If you do, you might end up lame for the rest of your life. Do you understand?"

I nodded, pleased at the prospect of sitting up. But there weren't enough peas to shell or apples to peel. I love to read but, even though we had more books than most families, I had read them all before. After the first week, I wanted something besides *Holiday House* and *The Pickwick Papers*, much as I loved them. I grew weary of the little room off the parlour. I detested sitting like a giant doll while the others were free to run. When Hamish and Charlie moved into town to go to high school and Hugh went to the schoolhouse up the road, I grew frantic with longing to escape.

I suppose I made my misery all too plain. But I did not notice how fed up with me my family had grown until Granny took me to task.

"It's high time you gave up moping and got busy," she said.

"Busy with what?" I growled. "I can't move!"

"That tongue of yours is active enough," she snapped. Then she went on more gently, "You need something to take your mind off yourself, lassie. The Dominie tells us you could be an author like Miss Austen someday. Why dinna you write us a book to read in the evenings?"

"Me! Write a book!" I could not believe my ears.

"Mrs. Traill and her sister must have been girls like you once upon a time," Granny said calmly. "Jane Austen too. And the author of *Holiday House,* come to that. I'm sure they began scribbling down stories when they were no older than you are now."

"What could I write about?" I said, startled but pleased with this wild notion.

"Why not your own story?" she said, surprising me again. "You hae done a mickle lot of living for a maid in her sixteenth year."

I saw at once that she was right. But paper was scarce and expensive and I would need a lot if I were to write a whole book. Granny read my mind. She has always been good at that. She left me to think while she fetched a big ledger that had belonged to Grandpa Ross.

"I brought this all the way from Glen Buchan," she said with satisfaction. "Molly thought me daft but I had a notion it would come in handy. Your grandfather died before he wrote a word in it. You can use it for your book. And here's a new pen from your mother. She thinks your writing a book is a grand idea. She'll be in to tell you so when she's done making oatcakes."

It sounded as though the thing had been decided.

"I'll need ink," I said feebly, staring down at the big book lying on my knees.

Granny produced a corked bottle from her apron pocket.

"Here's a pot I made for your father to write up his accounts. He's only half through the last bottle. Now let me hear no more excuses. You can make a start before Hugh comes in from school."

I gazed at the riches she had provided and thought about my own story. It was unlike any I had read before.

Would anyone really want to hear it? I would have to start with my earliest memories of life with Mam at the Blacks' boarding house in Aberdeen. Jeanie Mack would play an important part too. What would she say to being in a book?

Shyly, I glanced up at Granny.

"Do I have to stick to things I know for sure? I can't remember every word folks said. I was just four when I left Aberdeen."

"Make a good story of it," Granny Ross said. "And dinna leave out bits because somebody else might not like what you say or remember it differently. You need lots of strong colours to make a good quilt, not just pretty pinks and whites."

I knew what Granny meant. When she makes quilts, she pieces together odds and ends, scraps and rags, until even the dark bits help make a pleasing pattern. Our clothes are seldom bright and eye-catching since they have to stand up to hard wear. Yet Granny dyes some pieces and bleaches others to add variety to each quilt she fashions. But, even after she has changed oatmeal-coloured homespun to a sunny yellow with onion skins or used berries to turn a faded pink into deep rose, I can always tell what the original looked like before she worked her magic.

So I am going to try to piece together my story. I want to put it down and see the pattern. I, too, may add a little dye now and then. It won't be as fine a book as one penned by Jane Austen, I know, but it will surely help me to pass the long hours.

The birthing room is the perfect place to be while I am writing. My book will be delivered where Ruth was born. Granny was the midwife when the baby came. She's been the midwife for this story too.

I plan to think each chapter through carefully before I begin to write so I will not have to erase too often.

Here begins the story of Elspet Mary Gordon, who was born Elspet Mary Iveson on January 2nd, 1832, in the city of Aberdeen, Scotland, and of how she first became an orphan and then found a new family and travelled with them to a far country where she found, at last, her heart's home, the place where she belonged.

1

The Day Mam Did Not Come

*U*ntil I was almost four years old, my mother and I lived in a little attic room on the top floor of the Blacks' lodging house in Aberdeen. Mrs. Black's little girl Jemima was the same age as I was and we loved playing with each other.

One rainy afternoon in late November 1835, Mam said, "I must go out and buy food or we'll have no dinner."

I did not enjoy shopping with my mother. She walked too fast. She would not pause to stare at raindrops on an iron railing or watch kittens playing or study her reflection in a puddle. She was always in a hurry.

"Can I stay and play with Mima?" I asked.

"I'll see if Mrs. Black can have you," she said. "I can be back quicker without you along, Elspet Mary. Never was there such a bairn for dawdling."

"Of course she can stay with me," Mrs. Black said, beaming at me. "Jemima will be over the moon. She's been begging me to get Elspet down to play."

Mam laughed and bustled away. I did not even watch her go. After all, I believed she would soon be back and I did not want to waste a moment of my playtime with Mima. I had no idea that I would never see her alive again.

Mima and I were so busy with our game of Fathers and Mothers that I did not notice the hours passing until I heard Mrs. Black's anxious voice murmuring, "Oh, I hope nothing's amiss."

I glanced over at her, my attention caught for the moment.

"Is Mam coming?" I asked.

"She must be coming soon," Jemima's mother said, peering out one of the small glass panes in the front window. I went and stood on tiptoe to see if I could glimpse Mam rushing down the street, but I did not see hide nor hair of her.

"Elspet," Mima called, "come back at once, you naughty child, or I'll give you a whipping."

I ran back to our game, anxious to play it out before my mother returned to fetch me away. But dusk fell and she still had not returned. Just as I was beginning to grow uneasy, Mr. Black came home from his work at the livery stable.

"Don't take your coat off, Stewart," Mrs. Black said. "You must go and see what you can learn about Mrs. Iveson. She's been gone for hours."

"Cannot it wait until I've had a bite?" her husband asked.

"No, it cannot. I've been driven frantic wondering what has happened to her. It should not take you long to get news. She was only going to the greengrocer and the butcher."

Grumbling under his breath, her weary husband stumped out into the driving rain. Jemima's Pa going out without a bite of supper told me something was seriously wrong. Deserting Mima, I tugged at Mrs. Black's skirt.

"Where's Mam?" I demanded, bursting into tears. "I want Mam."

She did her best to laugh.

"If she doesn't come soon, you can sleep here tonight with Jemima, Elspet," she said. "No more of that grizzling. I'm sure your mother will come back with Uncle Stewart."

I dried my eyes and ate my supper like a good girl. I still thought adults were too powerful to be harmed. Also, I was excited about sleeping at Jemima's.

Mrs. Black helped me out of my clothes and slipped one of Jemima's nightgowns over my head. It hung on me like a tent. My hands were lost in the long flannel sleeves. The hem lay flat on the floor. Jemima and her mother laughed.

"It'll have to do," she said. "But I'll tie a string around your middle and turn up those sleeves. You're such a bit of a thing next to our Mima."

She rolled up the sleeves and nipped in the waist with a length of twine. Although it looked better, Jemima and I could not stop giggling. Her mother gave us each a brisk slap on the bottom to quiet us.

"Kneel for your prayers," she said, seating herself on a low chair.

We knelt and rested our folded hands on her lap. We were careful not to look at each other in case we started giggling again. You did not laugh when it was time to pray.

Jesus, tender shepherd, hear me,
Guard thy little lamb tonight ...

I asked God's blessing for people I had never met, Mam's closest friend and sister-in-law Aunt Ailsa and her family, Uncle Thomas, Uncle Archie and Uncle Charles, and my father Rolf Iveson away at sea. I especially asked God to look after Mam, who seemed to be in some kind of trouble. I completed the list in much less time than Mima took rhyming off all her aunts, uncles and cousins.

"Help me to be a good girl," we both finished off. "In Jesus' name, Amen."

Mrs. Black put us to bed in Jemima's cot in the back room, Mima at one end, me at the other. After she had tucked us in, she went back to the window to watch for Mr. Black's return.

Jemima fell asleep at once. I could not follow her example. Mam always sang to me before I slept and lay beside me in the four-poster we shared. I felt cramped in the narrow cot and Jemima kept kicking. I was tired, though, and I had begun to yawn when Mr. Black's step sounded at the door. How slowly and heavily he walked! Mam should have been with him but I could not catch the sound of her familiar light footsteps.

Mrs. Black rushed to let her husband in. I strained my ears, intent on catching what they said.

"What news, Stewart?" Mrs. Black whispered.

"Mrs. Iveson's dead," Mr. Black said flatly, sinking into his chair by the cold hearth. "She was knocked down by a runaway horse. Her head struck a paving stone. She was dead when they took her up."

"The Lord have mercy on her soul," said Mrs. Black in a voice thick with tears. "She was just twenty-two and so bonny."

I listened to this much in frozen silence. Then I snapped out of my trance and began to howl. Mrs. Black rushed to the cot and picked me up. Quickly, so as not to rouse Jemima, she bore me into the front room and sat down, cradling me in her warm arms.

"I want Mam," I wept. "I want my Mam."

"I know, I know. She canna come right now. Rest, my honey. Hush," Mrs. Black murmured, rocking me back and forth and patting my back. She did not promise me that my Mam would be returning soon, but, when she tucked me in again, I had almost made myself believe that my Mam would be there, safe and sound, in the morning.

2

The Coming of My Da

When she thought I was asleep, Jemima's mother went back to the front room and she and Mr. Black picked up their hushed conversation again. The scraps I caught pulled me back from the edge of slumber and started me listening hard once more.

"Do you ken where her kinfolk can be found?" Mr. Black asked. "Who'll take the child now she's gone?"

"Oh, Stewart, if I hadn't forgotten the poor wee mite! We mun keep her with us until her Da's ship comes in. He mun decide what's to be done. I couldna put the bairn into an orphans' home."

"He may not come home for months," Mr. Black said slowly. "I dinna begrudge the child but we are not rich …"

"Even so, Stewart. We can manage. The child eats like a bird. I couldna sleep nights if she went to folk who were cruel to her. Think if it were our Mima!"

I put my hands over my ears then and willed myself into the safety of sleep. I would wake up, I felt sure, to find that Mam had returned after all and we would learn that we had been anxious over nothing. In the bright morning, the nightmare would be over.

But when morning came, the bad dream continued. At first, I kept running to the window to look for Mam but, as time passed and she did not return, I slowly began to face the truth. She would never come back to me. With my father away at sea and only dimly remembered, I, Elspet Mary Iveson, not quite four years old, was alone in the world.

I never again climbed the steep stairs to our small attic room. Mrs. Black must have slipped up there after we were asleep to fetch my clothes and pack up our few possessions. She kept Mam's tortoise-shell comb and brush and mirror and her amethyst brooch in a safe place, ready to hand to my father, but she produced my other dress matter-of-factly and saw that I wore it.

A cooper and his wife moved into our room the day after Mam was buried. Mr. Black thought I should be taken to the funeral but his wife spoke out against it.

"She's not yet four," she said. "She should remember her mother as a living, laughing woman."

But when Mrs. Black took us out of the house after that, she dressed me in a black frock which I detested.

"I do not want to wear that ugly thing," I said, glowering at her.

"You mun show respect for your poor mother," she said firmly and ended the discussion with a stern look that made it clear that I was being rude. Mam had never made me a black dress so I did not believe she would wish me to wear one. But I knew good children did not argue with their elders. Even though I mended my manners, I never felt like myself in that long-sleeved, high-necked, too tight, second-hand black dress. Whenever I was told to put it on, I felt like a sulky crow until I was allowed to change back into one of the two dresses my mother had made for me.

As days turned to weeks, I gradually stopped expecting to see Mam. The Blacks helped all they could, especially Mima. Only children as we both were, it was wonderful to have a playmate always at hand. Although I still missed Mam, I was too young to fully grasp the fact that she was gone forever.

"Where is she?" I asked often at first.

"She's in Heaven with our Lord," Mrs. Black said.

"I want to see her," I persisted.

"Be a good Christian child and you will someday," Mr. Black said gruffly.

He was someone who knew important things. He never teased. He was solemn and he made Jemima and me mind our manners. Even though I was a bit in awe of him, I knew he could be trusted. Wherever Heaven was, I would go there when I was big enough and my Mam would be there waiting for me. That was what I told myself whenever I felt grief washing over me like a gigantic sea wave threatening to pull me under.

In the meantime, I was with people Mam herself liked and trusted. "The salt of the earth," she had said of Mr. and Mrs. Black. I was safe with them.

Before long, I began calling Mrs. Black Ma just as Mima did.

"You're like my own bairn," she told me often. "Jemima and I will be lost without you when your Da comes."

Her mention of my father made me uncomfortable. Even though I still prayed God would bless him, I did not really know who this "Da" was. He was a bosun on a merchant ship which had sailed over a year before. I felt I belonged with Ma and Uncle Stewart. They often said Jemima and I were like twins.

Although Mima was a solid, red-cheeked child while I was small and pale, I wished passionately that we really were sisters.

Yet while Jemima called Mr. Black "Pa," he always made me say "Uncle Stewart."

"No sense in raising false hopes," he muttered.

Da's ship did not return to Scotland for another five months. Since we had waved goodbye to him, he had sailed halfway around the world. He came as soon as his ship docked and he got someone to read him the letter Mr. Black had left for him at the shipping office. He arrived at sundown.

Jemima and I were eating our bread and milk when he knocked. His seaman's hand was heavy. The knocking resounded like claps of thunder. I nearly upset my bowl and Jemima shrieked with fright.

"Hold your whisht, daftie," Mrs. Black told her. She got up from the table and went to the door. Mr. Black was not due home from the livery stable until after dark. But nobody who meant us harm would hammer on the door that way. The man who stepped across the threshold was so tall his head seemed almost to touch the ceiling.

"Here's your father at last, Elspet," Mrs. Black said quietly.

I stared up at Jemima's mother and the tall stranger. Her eyes were wet and she sounded like Jemima when she had a cold in the head. Something about this man had upset her. Shaken by Ma's choked voice, I was set to cry too when I realized what she had actually said. The giant standing just behind her was my father.

I studied him doubtfully. His face was very brown from the sun. His hair was fair and his eyes were bright blue. My eyes were the greenish-brown folks call hazel. But my short, straight hair was as flaxen fair as his. Was he really my Da?

I was still puzzling over it when he smiled. Then I saw his gold tooth wink. I had seen that flashing tooth before. Slowly I smiled back.

"That's my girl," he said in a deep voice I recalled at once.

He picked me up and gave me a hug and a prickly kiss. I rubbed my face against his cheek and laughed shakily.

"She was just two when I sailed. Now she's turned four. It's hard to get used to," he said huskily.

"It must be," Mrs. Black said, blowing her nose.

"Her eyes are so like her Mam's," he told her. Then he went on a bit roughly. "The day after tomorrow, I'll have the loan of a horse. I'm taking her to her Mam's people. I've paid for a letter to be sent to say we're coming. Can she be ready by then? I'd like to set out early in the morning and reach Glen Buchan the same night."

"Of course. We'll miss her," said Mrs. Black. "It will be a long journey for such a mite."

"I know, but I have only a week before I sail again. We'll stop to eat along the road. Her Aunt Ailsa will love her. Kirsty's brother William will make her welcome. He was fond of his sister. The child's not sickly, is she? She looks as though a breath of wind would carry her off."

"She just needs feeding up," Mrs. Black said. "She doesn't put on pounds like my Mima. Dinna fash yourself, Mr. Iveson. Once she's settled down with her aunt, she'll grow stout."

The next day, the Blacks and I were mournful. I was glad when bedtime came. Early the following morning, Mrs. Black made my spare clothes and a few small treasures of Mam's into a neat bundle. Da arrived just after sunrise. He wrapped me in my mother's big plaid shawl. I was a bundle myself. Only my face showed. Mrs. Black lifted me up and held me close.

Da tied my bundle on behind the horse's saddle. Then he unhitched the tall grey animal. He swung himself up onto its broad back. It shook its black mane and swished its long black tail.

I stared at it fearfully. Mam had been knocked down by a runaway horse. She had never come home. What if this were the very one who had done it? The thought made me shiver. I longed to run and hide.

But I did not. I waited, frozen with fear, for the beast to charge off down the cobbled street, tossing Da to his death.

"I'm set. Hand her up," my father said as calmly as though he were sitting on a kitchen chair.

He reached down. Mr. Black took me from his wife and lifted me up. Then I was safe in the crook of my father's elbow.

"Goodbye, Elspet," the Blacks called. Jemima was crying.

"God bless you, my bonny wee lass," Mrs. Black sobbed.

"Thank you again," Da said. "Gid-up, old nag."

We were off. I was bound for a new, untried place full of frightening strangers.

3.

How I Arrived in Glen Buchan

*T*he morning my Da and I left Aberdeen, my hands were wrapped inside the plaid so I could not wave. I did not cry. I felt small and alone. What if Da let me fall? The horse jolted me up and down. It snorted and tossed its head again. Although it was really a mild old creature, I had never ridden on a horse before. It seemed enormous and wild to me.

Aunt Ailsa, I said inside my head. Aunt Ailsa will love me.

Mam had talked of this Aunt Ailsa. She had smiled and showed me pieces of paper filled with writing.

"It's a letter from your Aunt Ailsa," she had said, and her voice sang. I remembered because something had fallen from the letter. I had picked it up and handed it to her.

"What is it?" I asked her.

And Mam had sat down and taken the dried flowers into her hand and her eyes had filled with sudden tears.

"It's heart's-ease," she said unsteadily. "See the three colours? The white stands for love, the blue for memories and the yellow for souvenirs. Ailsa and I read a book on the language of flowers once so we could send secret messages to each other."

Spellbound by this glimpse of a mother I had never known, I had waited for more.

"Ailsa and I have been best friends since she was eleven and I was eight," my mother had gone on in a dreamy voice. "I started going to the village school that year. I was supposed to be delicate so they kept me home a year or two longer than usual. But I was fond of learning. I read as well as Ailsa and I could do sums in my head while the older ones were totting them up on their slates. In those years, we had plenty of love and happy memories too. Souvenirs ... I suppose you are my souvenir."

"What is ...?" I began, wrinkling up my forehead.

Mam's hand had clenched into a fist, crushing the pressed flowers so that they crumbled into bits. Then she rose to her feet.

"Never mind," she said. "Get your bonnet. We're going out."

She never spoke of the heart's-ease flower again. But it had been from the Aunt Ailsa we were going to see.

My father and I were clear of the great grey city before the morning was half over. It was a dark day with a scudding wind. Every so often, a gust of rain dashed over us and blew on over the hills. We trotted along muddy country roads. We passed small stony fields and hedges bright with spring flowers. I fell asleep after a while. I woke up when Da stopped at an inn. He handed me to a stable man.

"Good day, my bonny," the man said. He smiled at me. He had no gold teeth. He had no teeth at all. But he looked nice. I did my best to smile back.

Da got us some food. I drank half a mug of tea and nibbled an oatcake with a slather of heather honey on it.

"You should eat more," Da said. "You'll never make old bones if you pick at your victuals that way. Have a bit more."

I shook my head. I would be sick if I did. I did not tell Da but maybe he guessed. He did not press me further.

A kitchen maid took me out to the privy. She held up the big plaid.

"They've made you into a parcel," she teased, helping me to pull down the skirt of my dress. Then she wound the plaid around me again and carried me back to my father.

"You don't weigh as much as a feather," she said.

"Time to go, Elspet Mary," Da said, giving the maid a penny.

When I next woke, we were in a wild, lonely place. I did not catch sight of a single house. I saw low hills with grass blown flat by the wind. Birds called. The sun had pushed through the clouds and was painting them purple.

"You don't say a word. Can't you talk?" Da said.

I talked very well for my age. But I did not say so. I had a hard lump in my throat. I wanted Mrs. Black. I did not belong with Da. I was afraid of him. I was afraid of the big horse we rode. And I was afraid of the coming night. Even though I was warm enough in the thick shawl, I shivered.

"Faster, old nag," said Da. "My Elspet is cold."

His voice was kind and he gave me a little hug. I snuggled down until my mouth and chin were covered by the plaid. Da was just as nice as the man with no teeth.

"I'm warm," I told him softly.

The chill wind whistled around us. The horse's hooves clattered on the stones in the road. I felt sure Da had not heard me. But I did not try again. Talking on horseback was too hard.

Although my father's strong arm held me firmly, I knew he did not love me as Mam had done. Long ago, Mam had often held me close. I remembered how tender her clasp had been.

Then I saw the full moon. It was rising between two low hills. It had a round white friendly face. It seemed to smile at me. I tried to smile back but I was so tired.

Long, long ago, Mam had sung to me about a cow jumping over that moon.

"We're nearly there," Da said. "The village is just over those hills."

Was he talking to me or to the horse? I did not know. I tipped my head back so I could watch the friendly moon. I tried hard to keep my eyes open but my eyelids were so heavy. They closed in spite of me. I started to slide back into sleep.

"Whoa!" Da called.

The horse stopped. My eyes flew open. Da and I were in a village street. Nobody was about so it was late. Firelight shone in the windows of the clustered houses. I gazed about me, frightened but also excited. I was sure I had never been out so late before.

Then the door of the nearest cottage was flung open. A man and a tall boy came out. The man was carrying a lantern. He lifted it high and peered up at our faces. I blinked at the sudden light.

"Yes, William Gordon, it is myself and the child," Da rumbled.

The man handed the lantern to the boy and took the reins.

"Welcome to Glen Buchan, Rolf. This is Ailsa's nephew Malcolm Ross. We've been watching for you," he said.

Da swung down from the saddle. He still held me. The other man smiled at me and touched my cold cheek with one warm finger. The fingertip felt rough but the touch was gentle.

"So this is Kirsty's little Elspet Mary," he said. "I was grieved to learn of my sister's passing, Rolf, but it is a joy to see her daughter at last. Kirsty wrote to Ailsa of the babe's birth, of course, and sent news of herself and the child twice or thrice since."

"Well, she'll be your Elspet Mary if you'll have her," Da said. "I canna look after a bairn, William. I'm a seaman. Sailing is all I know. And I have no kin in these parts."

"Come away in," the man said. "Malcolm can tend to your horse. Be sure to rub him down, boy."

Malcolm nodded and led the beast away. My uncle held the lantern up, lighting our path. "We can talk better by a warm fire. If we tarry, Ailsa will be coming to find us and the wind is sharp."

The moment we entered the cosy, firelit room, a lady, already on her feet, hurried to us and held out her arms. Da handed me to her with a small sigh. Despite her lace cap, I could see that her hair was a fiery russet and her eyes were deep brown.

"My poor poppet! I'm your Aunt Ailsa," the lady crooned, sitting down on the settle. She hugged me to her and then began unwrapping the plaid. She kept right on talking as her hands worked deftly. Her words enfolded me like another warm shawl.

"Och, you must be worn out. You must be hungry too.

I hope that father of yours remembered to stop for a bite and sup along the way."

I sent my father a fleeting look and nodded my head.

Da smiled at me but he was too anxious to get things settled to waste time on chat. His concern made him abrupt. "I can't stay long," he said gruffly. "My ship sails again in five days. I'm the bosun and I must be there. Will you keep her? I'll send money when I can."

"Of course we'll keep her." Aunt Ailsa held me tight in arms as tender as Mam's. "We've only got the two boys, Hamish and Charlie. She'll be my girl, won't you, Elspet? I was just needing a little lass to love. She belongs here, Rolf. We're her family. Not only was Will Kirsty's brother, but she and I were like sisters ever since I was eleven and she was eight."

The boy Malcolm came in quietly. He tried not to stare at me but could not help himself. I was too sleepy to understand all that was said. Yet, when I grew older, I thought my new life began with that long ride through the darkness, the moon's smile and Aunt Ailsa's hug. The gentle music of her loving words made my heart sing.

"She belongs here. She belongs with us. We're her family."

This, I thought as I drifted into a deep, healing sleep, must be my belonging place.

4

"She's Mother"

I opened my eyes and gazed around the small, dim room in which I found myself. I had never seen it before. An old lady, with a face like a walnut under her white cap, sat next to the high window in a rocking chair. She was busy mending a jagged rip in the knee of a boy's breeks. She did not notice, for a moment, that I was awake.

When she saw me staring at her, she gave a little nod.

"Well, lassie, so you've joined the land of the living at last," she said. Her voice was brisk but it held a clear welcome. "I'm Granny Ross. I knew your mother when she was a bairn like you."

"My mother?" I echoed, gazing in wonder now.

The lady nodded again.

"She was flighty even then and a handful but she could charm the birds off the bough. You've not got her black hair but you surely hae her eyes. All the Gordons hae those bright hazel eyes. Are you famished, my honey?"

I blinked, yawned and sat up.

"Are you my Granny?" I asked hesitantly, not yet ready to think about breakfast.

"Your Da's mother died, I believe, when he was but a babe. Your Mam's mother lives not too far away. But I daresay you'll be calling me Granny along with the rest of them in this house. I'm your Aunt Ailsa's mother and my home is with her just as yours is going to be. I'll tell her you're awake. How about a bowl of porridge? That'll stick to your ribs."

I grinned at her. My mother had always said that about oatmeal porridge too. I knew it would fill up the emptiness inside me.

"Yes, please, Granny," I said shyly and hopped out of bed.

Granny Ross and I were fast friends from that moment on. Perhaps it was because, small as I was, I was handy at running errands and felt important lending a hand. Perhaps it was because we had both come to the Gordons' household from elsewhere.

When her husband, the village schoolmaster, had died two years before, Granny Ross had had to move out of the cottage that went with the school. She had come to live with her youngest daughter Ailsa and her husband and children. Because her own life had been turned upside-down not too long before, she understood how I felt during my first weeks with the Gordons. She helped me sort out all my new relations and came to my rescue when I felt lost among so many strangers.

It was not easy for me to fit in. Hamish, recently turned seven, and Charlie, five and a half, were bursting with energy and full of mischief. I watched them with alarm and fascination. Mima Black's charms paled when set next to their rowdy toughness and high spirits. Mima and I seemed so sedate in comparison. I had been all my mother had to love and she had pampered me more than a little. And she had never had any reason to introduce me to boys.

Mam, for all she loved me dearly, had had very little money and so I was not used to many sweets or playthings. What the Gordons had, in their crowded cottage, seemed untold riches compared to the little Mam and I had had in our attic.

I called the old lady Granny with no trouble but it was hard for me to remember to say "Aunt Ailsa" when Hamish and Charlie called her Mother.

"You, Elspet, stop saying Aunt Ailsa," Hamish said finally. He sounded very grown-up to me. "She's Mother. That's right, isn't it, Mam? You're her Mam now hers is dead?"

Aunt Ailsa smiled down at me. Even her eyes smiled.

"It's up to Elspet," she said gently. "How would you like Hamish and Charlie to be your brothers instead of just your cousins, my lamb?"

"A horse killed my Mam," I told my new brother importantly. "A big grey horse with a black tail."

Aunt Ailsa looked surprised but she went on quietly, "She was killed in a road accident, that is true. I never heard the horse was grey. But, Elspet, we were talking about what you should call me. You might like to say Mother or Mam the way my boys do. Your mother was my friend and I think she would not mind. I'd be so happy to be your mother since Kirsty herself can't be here with you."

Aunt Ailsa stopped talking and waited.

"Mother," I said softly, trying it out. "Mother."

"Yes, dear heart," said my aunt, whom I called Mother from that moment on. She stroked my hair tenderly. "That's the way."

Having acquired one Granny and been told I had another a few miles distant, I was curious about my second grandmother. Grandfather and Grandmother Gordon lived not five miles away, over the high hills.

I asked to go and see them but nobody heeded me at first. Finally, when Mother thought I was settled in, she took me on a formal call. We went one Sabbath after we had had our noon meal. The two of us drove there in my Mam's sister Aunt Molly's pony cart, which I loved. As the pony jogged along the dusty road, Mother tried to prepare me for what was going to happen.

"Your Gordon grandparents are elderly and no longer used to children," she said, choosing her words with care. "They may seem a bit … stiff. You must mind your manners whatever happens, Elspet Mary. Be a credit to your mother." This might have confused me but I was only half listening. Hamish had warned me I might not like them. But I did not care. It was an exciting thing to be taking a trip alone with Mother and riding in the pony cart.

She took a deep breath and then let it out in a sigh.

I would find out what my grandparents were like soon enough. Now I was singing under my breath.

I had a little pony.
I called him Dapple Grey.
I loaned him to a lady
To ride a mile away.
She whipped him. She lashed him.
She rode him through the mire.
I'll never lend my pony now
For any lady's hire.

I was sober enough when the song ended. Finally I asked, "Why did she whip him and lash him?"

"I don't know, my lamb," my mother said. "But she should not have been so cruel. There's your grandfather's house at the top of the rise."

I looked up at the dark, silent house and felt the first prick of unease. I inched closer to Mother.

"Maybe they won't like me," I whispered.

"Whether they do or not, you see that you are respectful," she began. Then she put her arm around me and hugged me, holding the reins with her left hand.

"We love you, Elspet. If the Gordons dinna see what a dear bairn you are, it's their loss," she said. "Now hold up your head and let's get the visit over with. Remember that they are old and they loved your mother when she was a child like you."

"Yes, Mother," I said as staunchly as I could.

I smiled up at her and waited for her to smile back. When she did not, I found that I, like Hamish, was afraid.

Not Like Us

Climbing down from the pony cart, I thought of what Hamish had said. "He gives me the shivers," my adopted brother had confided, after checking to see nobody else was within earshot. "He's forever going on about hellfire and quoting Scripture at me."

"Granny Ross quotes Scripture," I said.

"Not like Grandfather. He only trots out verses about sinners being punished. Then he looks at me as though he can see right into my black heart."

I wanted to laugh but Hamish was not joking. I, too, often had quaked at the thought of the everlasting fire that the Minister said burned the souls in Hell. Mam had never talked to me of it but Uncle Stewart had told Mima and me that we would burn forever if we were not good girls. Mother spoke gently, though, of a God who loved His children and forgave them. I had come to put my faith in Mother's God. I lapsed back into terror every so often, however, once the candle was blown out and I was alone in the fearful darkness.

Now, in broad daylight, images of hellfire had no power over me. I shook off my foolish fright. I still wanted to meet these strange relations, didn't I? I was especially curious about Grandfather who could so terrify a big boy like Hamish. And Mother was holding my hand. What could go wrong?

When we went visiting anyone in the village, we called out and then walked in without knocking, knowing we were welcome. Yet, once Mother and I had mounted the steep steps, she banged the knocker and waited.

A housemaid opened the door. She beamed at Mother.

"Good day, Sarah. How's your mother?" my mother asked.

"Mither's up and pleased as punch to have a boy at last," the girl said with a broad grin. "They've called him Will after your man. My Dad's like a dog with two tails."

My mother laughed. I tried to imagine Shep with two tails but I could not quite picture it.

An old woman's voice called sharply: "Sarah?"

"Come along in, Ma'am," Sarah said hastily. "I'm to show you into the front parlour."

"This is our Elspet, Sarah," Mother said, steering me ahead of her into the big hallway. "Miss Kirsty's little girl."

Sarah gave me a nervous smile but did not speak another word. Mother and I were shown into the stiff parlour. The tabletops looked so polished they might be brand new. The starched antimacassars on the backs and arms of chairs were as white as snow. The house, which had not only an upstairs but an attic, seemed enormous to me. It was a drafty place and nothing in it made me feel at home. Even the scant fire in the hearth was trying to go out.

Nobody was in the room. Mother crossed to two chairs standing side by each and we sat down. I had a dozen questions I yearned to ask but this did not seem to be the time.

Grandfather Gordon stalked into the room then. He barked a greeting at Mother and sat down with his chair turned so that he could not see me. I shot a glance at Mother, got a reassuring smile and plucked up my courage.

"Good afternoon, Grandfather," I said.

He did not turn his head or answer. In all the time we were there, my grandfather never once looked right at me or seemed to even notice that I was in his house. I felt nettled by such rudeness.

I was glaring at his back when my grandmother rustled into the room. She had on a black silk dress and her lace cap was prettier than Granny Ross's Sunday best.

"Ailsa, how nice ..." she fluted, in a trembling voice.

I thought she was not going to notice me either but she did smile nervously at the chair where I perched. After a moment, she even murmured, "Good afternoon, child."

"Good afternoon, Grandmother," I answered politely.

Then I slid off the hard, too-high chair and went to lean against Mother's knee. Although Grandmother spoke to me, she did not look straight at me either. What was wrong with them?

She was a little like one of our hens, I thought. A frightened, foolish hen. She fluttered about us throughout the visit, and spoke to Mother in a flustered near-whisper.

"Mr. Gordon is not having a good day," she said. "He likes to see your boys but he has never been able to forgive Kirsty."

"If Kirsty needed forgiveness, Our Lord has long since forgiven her," Mother said. "I have brought your grand-daughter Elspet Mary to visit you. Surely you are anxious to get to know her."

Grandmother was crumpling a handkerchief into a small damp ball. Her face turned a dull red and she bit her lips.

"Kirsty was a wicked girl to give us so much heartbreak," she said after a long, painful minute had ticked past. "We warned her ..."

"Elspet's mother is gone," my mother said, putting her arm around me. "It is time to forget the past, Mother Gordon. Kirsty may have been foolish but she was not wicked."

Grandfather gave an angry snort but did not turn his head or speak. Grandmother jumped like a startled deer and then babbled on, her words tumbling out in a confused rush. Her next speech was recited in a sing-song babble, as though she had learned it by rote and was afraid of forgetting a bit.

"Mr. Gordon says the girl should have gone to her father's people. He told William so the day he first heard. The Ivesons should bear the burden. She certainly looks like him. That hair of hers isn't like anyone here. It's so fair, almost white. Heathen-looking. She is not like us, Ailsa. Not a bit like us. None of ours has hair like that."

I saw Mother's lips tighten. She looked at my grand-mother for a long moment without answering. Her arm drew me even closer. Then she sighed and said quietly, "Elspet has Kirsty's eyes, Mother Gordon. Dinna ye see that?"

Then my poor grandmother buried her face in her hands and started to cry. Mother put me aside at once and went to her. She stood and patted the old lady's shaking shoulder.

"Elspet Mary, go along outside," she told me quietly. "You can play in the garden until it is time for tea. I'll call you."

I walked out the door, my back stiff, my head high. Sarah was in the hall. I knew at once that she had been listening and she knew that I knew. She grinned at me as though we were the same age.

"Follow me, dearie," she whispered. "Do you know Maggie MacTavish?"

I nodded. Maggie lived in the village and was just my age.

"She's my cousin," Sarah said with a broad smile. "Here's the way out. Tell our Maggie I sent my respects."

I nodded. Then I walked down the steps into the garden. Although everyone said I was old for my years, I would not turn five until January. It was lonely outdoors and there seemed to be nothing for one child to do. The flowerbeds were so neat I dared not pick a single blossom. At last I found a stone bench to sit on and I perched there sedately, telling myself one of Granny Ross's stories.

Too many were about orphans, however, babes set adrift in coracles, ugly little changelings taking the place of the true children of the house, kings' daughters raised as goosegirls. Nobody seemed to be in her proper place.

Grandmother Gordon's words about my being "not like us" and my fair hair looking "heathen" broke through and snagged in my thoughts like cockleburs. I had no idea, that afternoon, how her muddled, un-happy words would continue to haunt me. I just longed to go home.

"Elspet, come and have some tea," Mother called at last.

I walked toward her, a bit stiffly from sitting still for so long. She touched my cold cheek and then leaned down to kiss me.

"We'll go home as soon as I can manage it," she whispered.

The seed cake and tea were good. It helped that Grandfather ate his alone in another room. Yet, even though he was not with us, he managed to cast a dark shadow over the party. We ate without talking.

When we were on our way back to Glen Buchan, Mother tried to explain away my grandfather's coldness by telling me that he had always liked boys better than girls. But she soon faltered and was quiet. I was not fooled. I saw clearly that it had something to do with my Mam running away with my Da long before I was born. I knew, whatever had happened, my Mam had been good and loving and I was on her side.

We visited again two months later. Nothing had changed. We did not even see Grandfather that time. Later, I heard Mother telling Uncle William she would not take me back there without him and the boys.

"He's his own worst enemy, Ailsa. He has never forgiven Kirsty for running off with Rolf. Father forbade her to see him and she flouted his authority. He's a proud man," Uncle William said with a sigh.

"Cruel and stiff-necked comes closer to the mark, William. Kirsty and Rolf were married right and tight the minute they got to Aberdeen. Elspet's but a bairn. She knows nothing but good of her mother," Mother retorted, quick as a flash. "I'd have run off too from that bleak house. I don't know how you and your brothers bore it."

"You didn't know him until you were eleven and Kirsty eight. He changed when she grew so bonny. He adored her when she was Elspet's age. Later her beauty alarmed him and he was so strict that he drove her away. Next time you go to visit, leave Elspet here with Granny."

"I dinna fancy going myself," Mother retorted. "I feel for your mother but she should stand up to him."

"It's too late. Besides, she pities him. He blames himself for Kirsty's death in some way. My mother can do nothing to ease him."

I felt faintly sorry for my grandfather after that but I was glad to be spared visiting his cold house.

"You're lucky," Charlie and Hamish both said each time they were scrubbed and dressed up to go there for Sunday dinner.

"I know," I said.

Even though I soon fitted into the Gordon family as though I had been born to it, I still often ached with loneliness. When we went to the kirk, Granny sat me next to her on the hard pew and, if I got a tickle in my throat, she slipped me a peppermint or a humbug to suck. The service was long and dull and we had to sit up straight and listen so my throat tickled often. The Minister thundered about hellfire but I did not heed. I kept my face solemn and, inside my head, repeated the words of the Psalm Granny made us memorize every week. Nobody could worry when she was saying, "Let the hills clap their hands and the mountains sing for joy."

When I woke in the middle of the night, I would lie in my trundle bed next to the tall four-poster and I would not know where I was. The moment I whimpered, Mother would gather me into her warm arms and hold me close. She wore a nightcap but her hair hung down her back in a long, bright braid.

"Was it a bad dream, my honey?" she would ask.

I would nod although I was not sure. Maybe it was a dream.

"There was a grey horse," I would start to say.

But then I would grow confused. All I was sure of was the lost empty feeling inside me. And Mother would softly sing that emptiness away.

Ride a cock horse to Banbury Cross,
To see a fine lady upon a white horse,
Rings on her fingers and bells on her toes,
She shall have music wherever she goes.

Soon the huge horse in my nightmares became a white one with bells on her harness. She galloped over the

Scottish moors with me on her back. As I rode, chimes sounded and my horse and I floated effortlessly over the magical countryside in Granny's fairy stories. Then Mother would sing another song and I would drift into a deep, untroubled sleep.

"She's not like us," Grandmother Gordon had said.

Mother almost erased those words by telling me, over and over, that I was not only like them; I was theirs. Yet, deep in some corner of my heart, the cruel words still had power to sting.

Talk of Canada

I soon felt I had always been Ailsa and William Gordon's youngest child. Jemima Black and her mother faded into the mist of my earliest memories. Kirsty Gordon, my Mam, grew more real, however, as the family in Glen Buchan told me stories about her when she was a happy, mischievous child. Mother sang the songs Mam had sung long ago and showed me the heart's-ease flowers.

Not only did I have a new set of parents and two big brothers but lots of aunts and uncles and cousins. My favourite was Aunt Molly's boy Malcolm, who had been there the night Da and I arrived. Aunt Molly was often ill and Malcolm would be sent to stay with the Gordons for days at a time. Sometimes I felt he was the eldest of the boys rather than the youngest of Aunt Molly's.

He was twelve when I arrived and he was more patient with me than Hamish. He made me a wooden boat to sail in the burn and carved a funny flat-faced doll for me to cuddle.

One day, when the two of us were sitting by the burn watching minnows dart back and forth, he spoke to me of Mam.

"Your mother was beautiful," he said. He glanced at the younger boys who were playing nearby and kept his voice low. "I used to think she was the bonniest lady in the world. She was always laughing and teasing. And she sang like … like a lark."

I sat very still.

"I remember," I whispered. And, for one fleeting second, I heard her singing as though she had never left me.

Malcolm, seeing the sudden longing in my face, put his arm around me and gave me a rough but comforting squeeze.

"Aunt Ailsa sings the same songs," he said gently. "She loves you as though you were her own girl. Don't grieve, Elspet. You belong to us now."

I leaned against him and let the loneliness for my mother blow away like a rain cloud chased by a brisk wind.

Then, when I was six and a half, my Da's ship was lost at

sea. He had left word that, should he die, he wished me to be legally adopted by his brother-in-law William Gordon. They told me of his loss very gently. I did my best to feel grief for the father I only faintly remembered. But I could not make him seem completely real.

I had another father now—I even called him Father—and a family to go with him. And Mother was expecting a baby.

"Maybe the babe will be a girl," she said. "Then you'll have a sister, Elspet."

I did not tell her I did not want a sister. I was "the lassie" and "my bonny." I felt special. Hamish had told me that there had been two other children who had died. They had been babies, he said, not big enough to talk. They had caught diphtheria. One of them had been a girl named Fiona after Grandmother Gordon and the other a boy called Robbie.

"We were sent to stay with Grandfather and Grandmother Gordon and we couldn't come home for days and days," he said. "Mother was terribly quiet and sad until you came."

The new baby, Hugh, was born in the late autumn. Mother and Father named him Andrew Hugh but everyone called him Hugh from the start. I adored him. I would have given him the sun and the moon if he had wanted them. But he was a contented child who never cried for the moon.

"I love each of you equally," Mother told us older children, "but Hugh is, without question, the best baby."

Then, one December night at supper, Father began talking about a gentleman who had come to the mill and spoken with the men about the life they could be living in Upper Canada. This Mr. Adam Fergusson and his friend James Webster were thinking of financing a ship to bring Scottish settlers out to take up land close to a town they were founding near a place called Toronto.

Mother and Granny looked interested. We children were not really listening. We were excited about hogmanay coming. Upper Canada had no reality for us.

As the winter wore on, however, Father spoke several more times about Mr. Fergusson and his scheme. He read a book which the man had written telling all about homesteading. Finally, at the end of February, he shocked us by announcing that he and Uncle Thomas, his younger brother, were considering taking passage on Mr. Fergusson's ship.

Charlie and I were fully occupied feeding our old dog Shep under the table. We had to be very careful not to let Father catch us at it because Shep, a border collie, was a working farm dog and Father did not want him turned into a "spoiled house pet."

But Hamish was ignoring Shep.

"Do you mean we'd be going to live there?" he asked, his eyes bright.

"So far, we're just talking it over," Father said. "But you can have land of your own there for next to nothing. Thomas and I want to go and see if what we've heard tell of the country is true. You have to clear it, of course, and build yourself a cabin to live in. Your mother is ready to come out after we've settled on a homestead and built ourselves a log shanty. She's a brave woman, your mother."

"You're daft even to be talking of such a thing," Granny Ross snapped. "I canna credit it. Ailsa must have lost her wits to let you blather on that way."

"Nothing's decided yet, Mother Ross," Father said. He smiled but his voice had a steely edge. "Don't start scolding me as though I'm a laddie like Hamish. I'm past thirty and a responsible man."

"You have no more sense than Charlie if you're talking of leaving your ain folk and crossing the sea," Granny said, her voice even sharper than his. No answering smile warmed her eyes.

Crossing the sea? Those words caught my attention. Da had been lost in an Atlantic storm. I had thought Canada was a city like Aberdeen, far away but not on the other side of the ocean. Surely Father and Uncle Thomas would not go any great distance. They would be home in a week or two at most.

"Would you bring me a new hair ribbon from Canada?" I asked, putting my idea to the test.

He reached out and drew me from my stool next to him to sit on his knee.

"No, no, my honey," he said. "If we decide to try the venture, your Uncle Thomas and I will be gone for a year at least. We're thinking of homesteading. Once we're settled, God willing, I'll get work as a stone- mason. There is plenty of building to be done in a new country. We can get land cheaply if we'll work it and live on it. They want settlers so there are no taxes, not until you're established."

"But, Father, why …?" I protested feebly, not knowing where to begin.

My words were swept away as he talked on, his eyes glowing, his face flushed with excitement.

"When we'd made a fit place for you, I'd come to fetch you all away. We'd not be going for a visit and coming home with hair ribbons, Elspet; we'd be moving to Upper Canada to stay."

I stiffened. The half-forgotten lost feeling that had filled me when Da took me from the Blacks swept through me again. I loved my home in this village. I knew everyone. Everyone knew me.

I understood, if a bit vaguely, why Father wanted his own land. I had often heard them speak of his situation. Because he was the third son, he would never own the land he helped to farm. It belonged to Grandfather Gordon. Last summer Grandfather had had an attack of apoplexy and the doctor had told him he must hand over running the farm to Uncle Archie or he would be dead in a year. Grandfather had almost had another attack but, in the end, he had done as he was bid. He and Grandmother stayed in the big house but Uncle Archie, with Uncle Charles as his good right hand, had taken over managing the home farm. Father had always known this would happen and, although he had helped out on the land when the work was especially heavy and pastured a few sheep with Uncle Archie's flock, he had spent most of his time learning to be a stonemason with Uncle Robert.

Uncle Thomas, the youngest of the four Gordon sons, had become a carpenter's mate, working with yet another of the Gordon kin. Although they respected the older men, each brother hankered to be his own master.

"You're well enough as you are," Granny Ross told them whenever the younger men spoke of setting up for themselves.

Father had given her an unfriendly look but Mother had made him hold his tongue. None of us had seen that his discontent would someday cause him to uproot us all and transplant us in a foreign land. Now I realized that, when he had sat silently staring into the fire, Father had been looking not only at the leaping flames but into a changed life. He had also been seeing another place, a place where I would not belong.

He was the head of the house. The Bible said so. If he set his mind on going, we would all go, however we felt. I clutched his coat sleeve and cried out to him, willing him to take it all back.

"Glen Buchan is our home! We don't want to go away, Father. We know everyone here. We belong!"

Abruptly, he lifted me off his knee and rose from his chair. He strode to the door, snatching his cap and old tweed jacket off their peg as he passed. As he wound his plaid around his neck and shoulders, he spoke to Mother.

"I promised Thomas to meet some fellows at the pub," he said. "A man who's just come back will be there to answer our questions. We have a list of things to ask. He represents the man who's wanting to bring a boatload out. Don't wait up for me, Ailsa."

The door banged shut behind him.

"Elspet, you haven't finished your supper," Mother said quietly.

"He didn't hear me …" I wailed, not moving.

"He heard you, goosie. He just dinna care what a bairn like you thinks," Hamish said, laughing at me. "Oh, I do want to go. Why must we wait a year?"

Mother told him to keep mum and finish his pars-nips. I trailed back to my stool. I was not hungry but I picked up my spoon. I did not look at Granny. It would be no use. She knew the scripture about the man being the head of the house. Whatever Father said, I felt in my bones that he had already made up his mind. I did not think I could bear it.

7

A Grand Place

Nobody spoke to me about my outburst. Avoiding their eyes, I forced down two bites of bannock. It had no taste and I thought I might choke but I managed to swallow. Then I made myself look around at my family. Their faces were alight with dreams. Granny and I seemed to be the only ones who did not share Father's excitement. Charlie was as full of questions as an egg with meat. Hamish's eyes shone like torches.

"We'll see Red Indians," he shouted, "and hunt buffalo and bears."

"It's not decided yet, son," Mother tried to calm him. But her eyes, too, seemed to me to gleam more brightly than usual. I told myself I was imagining things. Surely Mother could not want to go away from the village she had lived in all her life. Then, to my dismay, I saw her smile, a smile bright with the same radiance that had set the boys and Father on fire.

Granny Ross, too, saw that smile and said nothing more that night. I was sure she was just biding her time. She would bring them to their senses. But time passed and she said nary a word.

In the next few weeks, the adults, plus Malcolm and Hamish, were forever arguing about emigrating. Some were for it, many against. But nobody kept quiet. Even the Dominie was thinking of going and the Minister, while he himself was staying where he was, preached about pilgrimages and Moses taking the Israelites to a new land. I detested those Israelites.

My big cousin Malcolm, now fifteen years of age and taller than Father, began pestering his uncles to take him along. He was still my favourite of the cousins and I tried to persuade him that none of us should leave Glen Buchan. But he was as deaf to my pleading as the rest.

"What in tarnation are you up to, coaxing the laddie to leave his hame?" Granny shouted at my father one night, breaking her long silence and glaring at him.

"We didna coax him," Father roared back, forgetting his manners for once. "He heard all about it from Ailsa and yon Hamish. But if we make up our minds to it and he still wants to come, I think it would be the making of him. Andrew and Molly have the older boys to help with the work and young Malcolm will be ruined if he's left to kick up his heels. We would have plenty to keep him out of mischief."

"He's an unco good laddie," Granny said, her voice softening.

"He was nearly caught poaching with Mikey MacTavish," Father told her grimly. "Keep that under your bonnet. He docsna know I ken what he's been up to. But if Molly and Andrew don't forbid him and he still wants to come, he's as welcome as the flowers in May."

Granny said not a word until Malcolm himself was eating supper with us a week later.

"Malcolm, why are you wanting to gang away from your ain hame?" Granny asked, watching him like a hawk.

I held my breath. What would he answer?

Malcolm Graham grinned at our Granny.

"Many hands make light work, Gran," he said. "You've taught me that. Uncle William and Uncle Thomas could use me. I know they could. And I'm itching to go. Please, Granny, give me your blessing or my mither and feyther will never agree."

Granny sniffed and sat still as a stone. At last, Malcolm could not bear it. He went and knelt by her chair and whispered something in her ear. She still sat unmoving and the only sound was the tick of the clock. Then she reached out a shaking hand, drew his head down and kissed him soundly.

"If you mun be going, you'll not gang awa' without my blessing, laddie," she said. "But I'll miss you sorely. I dinna want to lose you too."

For a fleeting instant, I thought of Grandmother Gordon. If she had said such loving things to my Mam … The thought was too difficult. I let it go and settled for being delighted Malcolm might be with us across the sea.

Father told the family, the following night, that he and Uncle Thomas had made up their minds to go with the settlers bound for a place called Nichol Township. None of us was surprised, but something was bothering me. I heard again what Granny had said to Malcolm. "I dinna want to lose you too."

"Granny is coming wi' us, isn't she?" I burst out.

There was a long silence which stretched on and on. Granny herself broke it, speaking in her usual tart tone.

"I might come later," she told me, "when you've got everything fixed up. I'm too old to blaze wilderness trails. I'll go to Molly's."

"What will happen to this house and all our things? We can't leave our house," I cried, still struggling to hold back the tide.

"The house belongs to Grandfather Gordon," said Father. "We'll sell what's ours lock, stock and barrel. We'll need the money to make a start. Uncle Archie is adding our sheep to his flock and Mr. Cooper will take the cow when I come back. You'll need the milk until then. Your Da left some money, Elspet. It'll go toward getting you a new home in the New World."

"But I don't want a new home," I wept.

"You will. Wait and see," Father said absent-mindedly.

He glanced at the door. As I saw him, I realized that he had been looking at it every few minutes for the last half hour. Mother, too, guessed something was afoot.

"Are you expecting a visitor, Mr. Gordon?" she quizzed him, smiling.

Then, right on cue, Malcolm burst in, his eyes sparkling.

"Father and Mother have given in at last. I'm to go with you."

Mother gasped and then beamed. Father stood up and clapped Malcolm on the shoulder. Granny tried to smile at him but began silently weeping instead.

"Granny, I can help Uncle Will," Malcolm started in a pleading voice. "And I can stay with Uncle Thomas next year when Uncle Will comes home for Aunt Ailsa and the bairns. Please, don't greet so."

"Dinna fash yourself," she told him, mopping away the tears and looking more like her usual doughty self. "I ken well you're set on going. It's just that I'll miss you."

"We'll miss you too, Mother," Mother said.

49

She meant it but the smile was still there in her eyes. The men made plans after that as though all of us were now overjoyed about the huge changes ahead of us. Nobody seemed to notice that I was not saying a word. I thought my father did not see how wretched I was. Then, the day before he left, he brought me an orange kitten.

"This is Furkin," he told me. "I rescued him from some farm louts who were busy drowning him. He'll keep you company while I'm away. You won't miss me one bit with him for company."

"I will." I flung my arms around his neck and did my best to swallow the great lump in my throat. "I'll miss Uncle Thomas and Malcolm, too, but I'll miss you most of all."

The following day was the Sabbath and we had to put on our best clothes and go to the kirk.

"I'll be home soon, puss," I whispered to the little cat.

We sat in our pew and listened to the Psalm. Even I, who usually daydreamed in church, was drinking in every word this time.

"If I take the wings of the morning and dwell in the uttermost parts of the sea, even there shall Thy hand lead me and Thy right hand shall hold me," thundered Mr. Barrie, the Minister.

It was comforting to know that, wherever the ship took Father, Uncle Thomas and Malcolm, the Lord God would be with them, watching over them every minute. My hand stole into Mother's and the two of us smiled at each other from inside our Sunday bonnets.

Once April came and the three travellers had ridden off in the stage-coach, Furkin did help comfort me. Whenever I had no task to do, I played with him. I taught the baby to be gentle with him and kept him safe from Charlie's teasing.

It was a long time before we had word from Father. The men left in May and the first letter didn't reach us until September. It had taken them seven weeks to get to Canada. Father wrote of his and Uncle Thomas's getting the deed to two hundred acres of land.

"Our acres are in the township of Nichol," Mother read. "The big house, when we build it later on, will stand atop a hill looking over a broad valley with a stream running through it. But we have much work to do before that house will be aught but a dream. Most of our land is covered with dense forest. By the time this reaches you, we should have cut down some of it and completed a log shanty."

We waited eagerly for more. Even I was interested, although I pretended not to listen. I still did not want to leave home.

No ships sailed from October to April so we knew there would be only one more letter before winter closed in. It reached us on the first of October.

"It's rough and ready here," Father wrote, "but you'll love it. The wildflowers are beautiful, Ailsa, and the forest is splendid. There is a lot of work to be done. Malcolm can hardly wait to show off his bulging muscles and he's as brown as a berry. Our boys will soon learn what real toil is. Yet it is so much better working for yourself."

"I already know what real toil is," Charlie complained, flexing his arm and feeling along it for a hard bulge which was not there.

"I wish I'd gone with them," Hamish said in tones of longing.

"Does he say anything about me?" I asked.

"Give Elspet Mary my love," Mother read out.

I stroked Furkin and thought about that. Father loved me. That was fine. But where was the bit about what I would do in Upper Canada? Would I have no special place? Were boys the only ones who counted? My friend Maggie MacTavish's father said such things, but never my father.

I was quiet until the next morning when Maggie came to the door to walk to school with me.

"Elspet, my father is talking of going to America now," Maggie said. "My mother says it's like a fever among the men ever since the Murdochs and the MacNaughtons and your menfolk went."

My heart lifted. I had known Maggie ever since she had come to live in the village. Canada would be a friendlier, less strange place if Maggie were there too.

"Will you be near us?" I asked eagerly.

"No," Maggie said, her face doleful. "My father wants to go to Nova Scotia. He likes the sound of it better than the place where your folk are. We have cousins there too. But I think the MacPhersons are going with your kin, and maybe the MacIntoshes."

"Oh," I said dully. My steps slowed so that Maggie had to tell me to get a hustle on or the Dominie would stand us in the corner for being tardy. I hurried. But the families she had named had no girls my age. Until that moment, I had not stopped to think I would be losing not just Granny and the village but Maggie and the other girls I knew. Father's letters said not a word about girls. He did not mention a village or even one family of neighbours. I felt more uneasy than ever.

If it had not been for Furkin, it would have been a sad year.

Later I remembered what Maggie had told me.

"Mother, why doesn't Father say anything about the village?" I asked. "He has not told us one word about other children."

"Cheer up, dear heart," Mother said. "He's a mere man. He has no idea how much neighbours matter to you and me. But there will be neighbours, I'm certain sure. It will be a grand place."

"I hae my doots," I said darkly, imitating Granny Ross. "And even if it is grand, it won't be our place. I'm sure I'm going to hate it there."

"If you look for thorns instead of flowers, you'll live in a wilderness of your own making," Granny said sharply.

I stared at her. What did she mean?

"Close your mouth, child. You look like a simpleton," she said.

Mother smiled at me over Granny's head.

"Elspet will see the flowers, never fear," she said.

I was not sure what they meant but I made up my mind to puzzle it out later. And, whether Nichol Township was filled with flowers or thorns, I still wanted to stay in Glen Buchan.

8

"It's Father!"

*T*hat year without Father and Malcolm crawled by. We missed Uncle Thomas too but he had not been with us daily as the others had. Finally spring returned and we knew Father would be coming as soon as he could get passage. Still we heard nothing until late one afternoon in June.

I was sitting at the table eating a scone in a ladylike manner and watching my brothers gobble theirs like starving wolves. Hamish helped himself to his third before I was halfway through my first.

"You are a pig, Hamish," I said mildly.

He ignored this as I knew he would.

"The first thing I remember," he said, with his mouth full, "is old Shep stealing my scone. I was just three and he was as tall as I. He plucked it right out of my hand and I yelled. I thought Father would be angry with Shep but he roared at me to hold my whisht. 'God loves a cheerful giver,' he said."

Shep had died six weeks after Father left. Even though that had been more than a year ago, we all still missed him sorely. We all laughed at the look on Hamish's face as he told what Father had said. Then Charlie spoke quickly before anyone had a chance to grow sad.

"I remember falling through the ice on the burn and Grandfather Gordon pulling me out. He roared too. Bellowed like a bull."

"That's no way for you to speak of your grandfather, laddie," Granny Ross said sternly. She shot a glance at Mother as she spoke. She thought Mam was too easy on us.

Licking the butter off my fingers, I thought of my Da bringing me here one moonlit night and how Mother had said I was her little lass. While I held that precious moment in my heart, Hamish stood up and stretched. Then he sauntered over to the window, parted the stiff net curtains and peered through the glass. The next instant he whirled about, his eyes blazing.

"It's Father!" he shouted. "Father's come home!"

As my big brothers dashed out the cottage door, I ran to take Hamish's place at the window. Could he be right? He had keen eyesight but could he pick Father out from that distance, after so long? My eyes were wide with mingled alarm and excitement as I gazed up the hill to the crossroads. That was where the stage-coach set down its few passengers.

The coach was certainly there. I too saw its bulky shadow clearly. Our village had only the one cobbled street with the church, the shop, the public house, the school and the cluster of low cottages lined up along it. I, staring through the window, paid no heed to the spitting rain which kept blowing in gusts down the street. It was Saturday afternoon but the cold had kept folks indoors. A handful of men had gathered to greet the coach. Only one passenger had jumped down.

The tall, lanky man stood with his bundle on one shoulder. He might be Father. He was looking about and greeting old friends. Father would do that, if it were he. Father had been gone so long. I did not know for certain until I saw Hamish, his dark hair blowing wildly, rush up and pump the man's hand up and down. Charlie, a year younger, arrived seconds later. He was not the eldest son so he did not have to be polite. He threw his arms around Father's waist and hugged him instead.

I saw my father throw back his head and give a great laugh at something one of the boys said. I stared at his profile in astonishment. He had a big bushy beard. He had had no beard at all when he had left Scotland.

"It's Father. But he has a beard," I said in a soft, anxious voice.

Mother did not answer. I heard the door bang again and was not surprised to see her go flying up the street after the big boys. Father waved his hat at the group who had met the coach. Then he came striding down the cobbles toward our mother. Hamish and Charlie skipped along, trying to keep up.

Now Father had his free arm around Mother's shoulders. Her face shone. Her cap had come loose from its pins and slipped down over one ear but she had not even noticed. She looked so happy that I felt shy watching. I turned away from the window, my fair braids swinging forward, my heart pounding with excitement. I glanced over at Granny Ross and made myself swallow the wild shriek I longed to give. Granny would not approve of shrieking.

The old lady had not moved. Her back, ramrod straight as always, did not touch the back of her chair. She still sat close to the fire. She was knitting a stocking for Charlie, who wore gaping holes in his hose as fast as she knit him new ones. Hugh was sound asleep in his cot. I could hear him sucking his thumb. He could sleep through anything.

"That wee lad will miss the last trump," Granny said often.

Furkin remained curled up on the hearthrug, his tail over his triangular pink nose, basking in the unaccustomed peace.

"It really is Father, Granny," I said. "He's got his arm around Mother. But he's grown a bushy beard."

"I ken who it be," my grandmother said tartly. She kept her needles clicking as though nothing had happened. "He'll be here in short order. No need for the whole town to watch us greet the man. Such an uproar is unseemly. Your grandpa had a fine beard when he was the same age as William Gordon."

I grinned. But beneath my excitement lurked an uneasiness I found troubling. Overjoyed as I was at Father's homecoming, I was worried that he might be planning to carry us off to his new world before I was ready. Surely he would not rush us. He would need time to recover from his long sea voyage, wouldn't he?

"Do you think he'll be wanting to go back again at once?" I began.

Then the door opened and William Gordon hit his head with a resounding crack on the low lintel.

"Now I know I'm home," his deep voice said. "In our cabin, I've made the doorway a foot taller."

Hugh's eyes opened at the sound of the deep voice and Granny's knitting needles were still at last. She gave her son-in-law a flashing smile. I was glad I had caught it before my grandmother's face grew sharp and stern again. Granny smiled at me more than she smiled at anyone else but still her smiles were rare and not to be taken for granted.

"Greetings, Mother Ross," Father said then, minding his manners.

"Welcome back, William Gordon," Granny Ross said, laying aside her knitting and letting her cheek be kissed. "There now, you've roused the bairn. It's your father come home again, Hughie."

Father looked down into Hugh's wide eyes and chuckled. He swung the two-year-old up and held him high so that his dark head touched the rafters.

"It's your old dad right enough, my Hugh," he said. "Give me a kiss."

Hugh, not at all shy, gurgled with laughter and obediently kissed the bearded cheek. Then my father spotted me still standing by the front window. I was studying him with wide, serious eyes.

"Well, Elspet Mary, do you think you'll know me next time we meet?" he teased.

I remembered the teasing voice but the lean brown face with its growth of beard looked strange to me even yet. Still, I knew I was not behaving well. I was delighted to see him. I should have run to him like the boys.

"Welcome, Father," I said primly, going forward to kiss him.

He looked into my eyes and must have seen my love for him shining there. Before I could step back, he gave me a bone-crushing hug. When I squeaked at the strength of his grip, he released me and laughed again.

"I left behind a bit of a bairn and, while my back was turned, you've sprouted up into a great giant of a girl," he said. "You canna really be my little Elspet Mary."

I laughed at his words but some of my muddled feelings made the laughter sound forced. He studied my averted face with a questioning look but when I remained silent, he turned to Mother.

"Lass, I'm faint with hunger," he said. "Do I smell fresh scones?"

Granny snorted.

"You may be hungry, son-in-law. I hae my doots about your being faint," she said. "Pioneer life has done you good, put meat and muscle on you."

Father sat down on the other side of the hearth. Mother hurried to bring him a plate of scones and a bite of cheese. They would keep him from starving while she got supper. I watched Father eat. I did not see any great change in him except for that beard. He gobbled down scones even faster than Hamish did. I still felt unsure of him.

Furkin, wide awake now, leaped to safety atop the clothes press. He clearly did not recollect this man. He did not now remember himself as a scrawny kitten. He no longer remembered being saved from a gang of rough boys bent on drowning him and brought to me. But I, for once, was not paying any mind to my cat.

What had Father said about a cabin with a taller door?

I knew what he had said. I even knew what his words had meant. Mother had read both his letters aloud, after all. He had found the land, built the cabin and come back to fetch us, just as he had said he would.

And I, his Elspet Mary, was still the only one who did not want to leave Glen Buchan. But even I knew, by now, that we were going. I watched my father finishing his supper and could not eat my own. I had to know the worst.

"Can I take Furkin?" I said in a whisper.

"I beg your pardon, Elspet Mary," Father said, frowning a little. He did not like his children to whisper when they wanted something. I knew that. I tried to speak up.

"Can I take Furkin?" I said, my voice sounding too loud now.

"Who is Furkin?" my father said.

I gaped at him, unable to believe he really did not remember. Then Furkin jumped onto his lap, reminding him who Furkin was. Father smiled and smoothed down his ruffled orange fur. The cat arched his back against the hard fingers, loving his firm touch, but Father himself did not look happy now. He sighed before he answered.

"I'm afraid not, lassie," he said at last. "He wouldn't like to go so far. Cats like places where everything is familiar. I'm sure Granny will care for him and we'll get you another puss."

I wanted to howl. I turned to the door, my eyes blinded by tears. Furkin, on Father's lap, purred like a kettle on the boil, not guessing he would soon lose me.

"Come, come, child," Granny said sharply. "You aren't thinking of going off and leaving me without so much as a cat to keep me company? I promise I'll cosset the creature. Now run out and bring in the things on the line before they get soaked."

I ran out the back door. Tears spilled down my hot cheeks. I let them flow for a few minutes. Then I knew I had to go back. I wiped my eyes and looked at the clothesline.

It was empty.

9

Getting Ready

I sat, with Furkin on my lap, and tried not to cry. The two of us were hidden from the house in a grassy hollow in the midst of a thicket of broom. But we could hear Granny singing.

Speed, bonny boat, like a bird on the wing.
"Onward," the sailors cry.
Carry the lad who's born to be king
Over the sea to Skye.

Why did Granny have to sing about crossing the sea? I gulped down a sob. How could I leave Furkin? No other cat could take his place. No Canadian cat would be this soft or purr so loudly.

"You're mine," I sniffled, stroking his fur while my tears plopped down onto his back. "You will miss me so terribly ..."

"Puss, puss, puss," Granny called, interrupting her song.

Furkin leaped off my lap and vanished through the broom. He did not look back. He knew Granny had a treat for him and, when Granny called in that special sing-song voice, he had no time to waste on me.

I gazed after him. Granny loved him almost as much as I did. Perhaps, if Father had let me take him to Canada, he would have pined for Granny.

I was getting tired of being the only one in the family who was not thrilled to be leaving Scotland. The boys talked of nothing but the journey. Father could not go two minutes without saying something about our very own land across the sea. Even Mother hummed while she packed. Everything had to be done in a rush so we would reach our new land before harvest. Uncle Thomas needed Father and the boys to help with the work Father talked about.

"Our help, too, Elspet. Wait and see," Mother murmured when my face grew sullen.

I got up and dusted bits of dirt off my skirt. I trailed into the cottage, pausing on the way to pick a stalk of heart's-ease. What was it about this weed that always comforted me?

I had a feeling I should remember. It had meant something. Mam had said so. Memories. That was part of it.

"It's no use taking winter clothes for Hamish and Charlie," Mother said, sorting through our clothing. "And it'll be years before Hugh could wear these. We'll take bolts of good strong cloth …"

"Mother, don't you really mind leaving Scotland?" My eyes were puzzled.

"I've never been anywhere, Elspet," my mother said, smiling at me. "You've lived in Aberdeen but I've never been farther than ten miles from our own front door. I grew up at the other end of the village, you know, in Uncle Andrew's house. Mother came from the Orkneys but I've never even been there since she has no kin left in the islands."

"But don't you love Glen Buchan?" I cried. "We belong here."

I could not explain to any of them but my panic had something to do with Da's bringing me here so long ago. Away from here, mothers were knocked down by runaway horses. Away from here, the world was filled with danger and loneliness. I still had nightmares once in a while about being carried off by someone whose face I could not see.

And we would have to cross the ocean. Da had gone to sea in a ship and had never returned. His ship had sunk in a bad storm. What if storms blew up during our crossing?

"What is it, dear heart?" Mother said, her eyes searching mine.

"Nothing," I muttered. I did not want her to be frightened too.

Turning my back, I stalked to the window. I stood there staring at nothing, trying not to think of storms and runaway horses.

"Elspet Mary!"

Mother sounded annoyed now. I jerked to attention.

"I've asked you twice to help me fold these blankets," my mother said, her voice softening. "Stop mooning about, child. We have a lot of work to do in the next three weeks."

I shrugged off my black mood and took the corners of the wool blanket and backed away, ready to help fold. It was no use trying to make them listen. Scots were a stubborn people. Granny said so. Granny should know.

"You'll like it when you get there," Mother said, taking the folded blanket and putting it with mothballs into the tea chest. "Try to be happier. Your moping is hard on all of us."

After that, I tried not to mope. But I could not eat much. Granny, who had nursed me through scarlet fever, must have grown worried.

"Perhaps she's too delicate," I heard her say one night. "I know you won't like the notion. But have you thought of leaving the child with me? Molly and I would take good care of her."

I went rigid. I did not want to go. But I certainly did not want to stay behind. Aunt Molly was kind but she was not Mother. Granny was not Mother either. Much as I loved my grandmother, I could not bear to be left in her charge. I held my breath and waited.

"I couldn't leave her," Mother said. Her voice sounded husky. "She's as dear to me as the boys and William. We'd all be lost without Elspet. Could you have gone off without me, Mother?"

"It's not quite the same thing, my girl," Granny Ross began.

"It's exactly the same thing," Mother snapped. She sounded as fierce as a tigress defending her cub. "Don't ever make such a suggestion in William's hearing if you value your life."

"William heard," Father's deep voice said from the doorway. "Elspet Mary comes with us. The change will do the lassie good. The sea air will put roses in her cheeks, Mother Ross."

I relaxed, and I stopped talking about not wanting to go. This was my family. I could not stand losing one of them. Even to be with Furkin and Granny Ross, I would not stay behind.

10

Goodbye, Furkin

*F*ather took the boys to say farewell to his parents. Mother sent a note to say she was sorry but she was too busy getting ready to leave. Father started to tell her she must accompany him and then let it go. Nobody mentioned me.

Afterwards, I heard Father telling Mother that Grandfather Gordon wished us well in our move to Upper Canada.

"He gave me twenty English pounds to help pay for whatever we need. It's a generous gift, Ailsa, you must admit."

"I said he was stiff-necked and cold-hearted; I never said he was tight-fisted," my mother said with a smile.

Two days before we were to set out, Granny Ross called me to follow her into the back garden.

"I want you to know that I'll take good care of the puss," she said. "I'll write to you about him when I can. You be a strength and a comfort to your mother. And do try to keep the corners of your mouth turned up, my honey."

I nodded, doing my best not to burst into tears on the spot.

"May God give you strength for whatever lies ahead, my dear wee bairn," she said huskily and marched back into the house.

That afternoon, she packed her box and prepared to move to Aunt Molly's and Uncle Andrew's. I was fighting tears again as I watched. She gave me an exasperated look from under her brows.

"For pity's sake, girl, save a tear or two until tomorrow. I'll be here to wish you godspeed," she barked. "It's only a step. I'll take the puss then."

Her old eyes glinted with tears when our wagon, laden with the possessions we could not bring ourselves to sell, creaked and jolted out of the village. I waved and waved. Tears streamed unchecked down my cheeks. I would not stop waving until long after Granny was lost to sight.

"You're a regular watering pot," Hamish grumbled, disgusted with me.

"Leave the lassie be, Hamish," Father barked. Then he took out his kerchief and blew his own nose like a trumpet.

It took us three days to get to the port. Then we were on the wharf ready to embark on an actual ship. I stared at its dark bulk with frightened eyes. Was this the same kind of craft that had taken my father to his death? The sails were furled, so there was nothing beautiful about the vessel. And there was nothing beautiful about where we were to spend our next weeks. We had no money to pay for a cabin above the water line. The three bunks, one above the other, in which we were to sleep, were narrow and hard and airless. The boys clambered up to the top one. Mother and I were in the middle and Father and Hugh were on the bottom.

It was good that Father had made the journey before because he had known how it would be. He had seen to it that we had brought provisions with us, oatmeal and tinned biscuits and potatoes and a little tea and sugar. We slept in our clothes and, although they were clean when we started out, they soon stank. Everything stank. It was noisy and I felt I could not breathe. The ship swayed even in harbour. In no time, I was retching.

"Not here, Elspet. Run to the rail!" Mother cried.

I dashed up the steep stair, one hand clamped over my mouth. Then I vomited over the side.

"Heaven preserve us," said a fat Irish woman, "the wee girl is bringing up her boots and we've not even set sail."

I was too miserable to feel ashamed. And, when the sails

were set and we were at sea, I was soon joined by a score of others, the fat lady being one of the worst. She did not even try to reach the rail but vomited freely in the crowded cabin, adding greatly to the sickening stench.

The ocean continued to heave up and down and so did my stomach. I was very seasick. Nothing helped. Whenever my insides felt like settling, I would think of Granny or Furkin and begin retching again. I could not picture them happy together. In my mind, each of them was separate, alone, lonely.

I was also frightened all the time in the first days. Nobody had mentioned my father's drowning to me. Perhaps they had forgotten. But I thought of it whenever the wind rose and whined in the rigging. I wanted to be comforted but I kept mum, believing that, if I spoke of my terror, the words themselves would bring on the storm I so dreaded.

"She's thin as a picked chicken," Mother said. "I'm worried about her, William."

"She'll get her sea legs soon," Father answered. His too-hearty tone did not fool even me. He was as anxious as she. There were good reasons for fear. Two infants and one elderly woman had died before the voyage was half over. The babies had been sickly from the first and Mrs. O'Brien had had a bad heart, Mother told us. But going on deck to attend their burial at sea sobered even little Hugh.

We were only a few days from our destination when the storm I had so dreaded finally pounced upon our little ship. First, late in the afternoon, the sky turned the colour of pewter. The sailors studied the clouds boiling over the horizon and crossed themselves as they raced to the rigging. We were all ordered below. What made it a nightmare was the darkness. In case of fire, every candle flame had to be snuffed and all lamps left unlit. The ship's timbers creaked as though she was going to come apart at her seams and the wind soon rose to a terrifying shriek.

"My Da…Was it like this for Da?" I shouted at Mother, my arms wound around her neck.

She could not hear me. She held me tightly against her, my cheek pressed to hers. I felt her lips moving in prayer. Charlie pushed close to us. Although he was nearly eleven, I felt him sobbing with fear.

"We're done for!" a woman screamed in the nightmare darkness. "Jesus, Mary and Joseph, help us!"

Then, over the noise of the howling tempest and the hysterical moans, my father began to sing. His strong voice rang out.

O God, our help in ages past,
Our hope for years to come,
Our shelter from the stormy blast
And our eternal home.

73

The blast still sent the ship plummeting down into the troughs between the giant waves. Yet, incredible as it seemed to each of us, the shuddering ship fought her way back to the rearing wave crests, time after time. Father's voice singing Isaac Watts's hymn, powerful as it was, came in snatches as his body slammed into the timbers against which he tried to stay braced. In moments, other voices took up the hymn. Perhaps he, like our Lord, had power to charm the wild wind, because before he had begun the next hymn, the storm started to abate ever so slightly and my panic eased a little.

When, at last, the sea was calm enough for lamps to be rekindled, I loosed my grip on Mother's neck and realized, with a start, that I was glad to be spared not only so that I could go on living but so that I could see, for myself, this grand country Father was so excited about.

In the next days, Father completed my cure. He carried me up and down the sloping deck wrapped in his plaid. I saw whales one day and icebergs twice. In spite of missing home, I began to perk up. I couldn't help it. When I actually asked for another cold potato one morning, the anxiety left Mother's eyes.

"We're going to make it there safely, God willing," she said, "but never ask me to make this journey again. We must succeed, William. The children and I couldn't go through this twice."

Then, one afternoon in July, we sighted land.

I stood at the rail. I stared across the green-grey billows at the blue smudge on the horizon. For once, I was as excited as Hamish. It had been so long.

The ship had not gone down in a storm. My whole family was alive and off the shore of Nova Scotia. God had not forsaken us, after all. And, before too long, we would be reunited with Uncle Thomas and my dear cousin Malcolm.

"Oh, my Elspet. We are going to set foot on solid land at last," Mother said. She sounded as though she were singing.

"No more hard tack," Hamish sang out.

"No more filthy water," Charlie joined in.

"No more being kicked black-and-blue by young Hugh," Father joked, tousling the little boy's dark curls.

The other passengers laughed aloud. Everywhere children began to cheer and caper about. Some of the cries were feeble and many of the excited children's faces were pale and pinched from weeks of illness and near-starvation. But nobody thought of this in the outburst of joy. We were on the edge of our new world and I found that I, too, felt suddenly filled to the brim with a wild elation.

11

Purrkin

*A*lthough the ship docked to get fresh supplies, the passengers did not stay ashore. Instead we spent more long days travelling up the St. Lawrence River. It seemed as big as an ocean and as rough at times. But, as we journeyed further up it, there was lots to see—little islands, occasional houses, children waving from wharves, thousands and thousands of dark crowding trees.

I could not believe in so many trees. There were no trees at all in Glen Buchan. I thought uneasily that those trees looked unfriendly. You could lose yourself among them. I shivered.

All of us were impatient.

"I'm sick to death of this river," Charlie burst out one day. "How much farther must we go, Father?"

Father grinned down at him and pulled his ear gently.

"Even after we land, we have a long trip ahead of us," he said, "and you'll have to walk many miles of it. You will wish the ship could have taken us all the way to Toronto."

"Not I," Charlie declared. "I'd far rather walk. I love walking."

"So would I," I said rashly.

"I'll remember that," said our father with a gleam of laughter in his eyes.

Finally the ship docked at Montreal. At long last, we were to leave her. Not one of us children was sad at the thought, although the adults were anxious about the cholera which had ravaged the immigrants stopping in the city. The captain assured everyone that the worst was over and that we need not be afraid as long as we were careful to stay outdoors and not lodge anywhere the disease had taken hold.

"Elspet Mary, let's go ashore and stay ashore," Mother said, smiling. She looked down at me past Hugh's dark head, as though she were waiting for me to smile back. I thought of Granny Ross telling me to keep the corners of my mouth turned up and I grinned in return.

Then we started for the gangplank. Hamish and Charlie ran ahead, pushing into the eager throng. I forgot to hang back. I dashed after them, slipped and came close to tumbling into the water.

"Slow down, lassie," Mother laughed. "We won't leave without you, I promise."

At that, Father caught me up in his strong arms and bore me safely across the hollow-sounding, bouncing plank. He set me down on solid ground and gazed around at all the bustle of a port city as eagerly as his sons were doing. Then, remembering me and my reluctance to make the journey, he bent down and spoke.

"Well, you are in Lower Canada now, Elspet Mary Gordon. You have arrived in the New World. How do you like it?"

I was too overwhelmed by the bustle and press to answer this sally. My big brothers stood near me, staring round-eyed at all the stone buildings, the crowds milling in the streets. I tried to walk to them, stumbled and almost lost my balance. The solid earth felt ex-tremely unsteady under my boots.

"Now you need your land legs," Father said, patting my shoulder. He waited for Mother and Hugh to join us.

"Wait here and stay together," he told us all, making the words an order not to be disobeyed. "I must go and arrange for our bags and boxes to be unloaded and brought to the stage-coach office. Keep a tight grip on young Hugh, Ailsa. Someone might make off with him if he wanders."

Leaving Hugh with eyes like saucers, he strode off to see to things. Mother snorted but her hand tightened on Hugh's skinny shoulder.

The five of us moved in a body out of the crush and stood waiting for Father's return. It was a boiling hot day. The noise of the harbour was deafening but exciting too. The wind smelled of fish and tarry rope and other things I could not place. A dark-skinned woman, with several baskets dangling from her arms and back, approached us.

"Buy a basket, lady?" she asked Mother in a soft voice.

Mother examined a large lidded one and, at last, bought it for next to no money. We children stared at the basket woman with eyes as wide as Hugh's. Until we left the glen, we had never seen anyone who was not white. On the ship, there had been some dark-skinned sailors but they had been Spaniards. Could this be a Red Indian?

"It is beautifully made," Mother said with a smile. Then she shot us a look that told us to mind our manners and stop staring.

"Was she a Red Indian?" Charlie whispered the moment the woman had moved off to show her wares to other passengers.

"She was brown, not red," I said.

"Do hush, all of you. Where could William have lost himself?" Mother snapped, hot and weary with waiting.

We quieted but our eyes followed the Indian woman as she moved about the crowd. Then, all at once and out of nowhere, a scrawny scrap of a black-and-white kitten came flying through the air. He landed, scrambling with tiny paws, on my boot toes.

"*Miaou!*" the little creature cried out.

"That man kicked him," Charlie exclaimed indignantly, pointing his finger at a great ox of a man.

The brute swore and shouted something about "I've had enough ill fortune in this benighted land. Get the unlucky beast away from me or I'll wring its neck."

But I did not wait for him to finish. I stooped, quick as lightning, and snatched the kitten out of harm's way.

"Poor puss," I crooned, glaring over his head at the cruel man.

As though he knew, at once, that I would save him, the kitten reached his little front paws up and clung to me. He was nothing but bones. He weighed less than a mouse. And he was hugging me just as Furkin used to do. Then he burrowed his tiny head into the hollow of my neck. At last, as I stroked him, he began to purr. His purr was incredibly loud for such a bit of a cat.

I smiled at the rumbling sound.

"You sound like Furkin," I said softly. "Don't worry, little one. I'll take care of you. Nobody shall hurt you ever again."

"Elspet, don't stand mooning over a puss," Hamish said.

His voice was rough but I knew that, if I chose to fight for the kitten, he would be on my side. Charlie and Hugh would be too.

"Put that kitten down, dear," Mother said. "Your father will be here directly. We have to get a wagon to take us to the stage-coach. We have a long way to go today. We cannot adopt a stray cat right now, however thin he is."

I set my jaw. I looked my mother in the eye.

"This kitten is starving and hurt. He's coming with us," I stated. "He's mine."

"Oh, child, have some sense," my mother said, tiredness sharpening her tongue. "We can't cart a cat along on a journey. As if Father and I haven't enough on our minds keeping track of you children …!"

"We might try," said my father, appearing from nowhere, followed by a man with a wagon. He startled me so much I nearly dropped my cat.

"You must be joking!" Mother declared, staring at him with cold eyes.

"We need a cat to keep the mice down, Ailsa. I was thinking we'd get one later but perhaps our Elspet has found the very kitten we need. Have you a name for him, lassie?"

"Purrkin," I said promptly.

"Well, it's up to you to keep him safe," Father said. "Jump up on this wagon now. Up you go, Charlie."

He helped Mother up too. She was not saying a word but we children all knew she was as mad as a wet hen. We sat meekly, eyes lowered, fighting hard not to grin. As Father was about to swing himself up, he leaned toward me and said softly, "No more cats, Elspet Mary, no matter how scrawny. My happiness is at stake."

I beamed at him. I felt brimful of joy. I had not felt such happiness spring up within me since the day Father came home and that was weeks ago. I held Purrkin tightly as the wagon swayed and jolted. The bony little kitten wriggled but he did not struggle to escape. He knew he was mine. He knew he was safe with me.

12

Blisters

As the wagon took us through the city, Mother sat stiff as a statue with the basket clutched in both hands perched on her lap. Her bonnet hid her face but I could tell she was still furious with Father and me. I stroked Purrkin's tiny head with one fingertip. How I wished she would get over it! She so seldom lost her temper that we were at a loss. Maggie MacTavish didn't turn a hair when her mother flew off the handle because she did it all day and every day. But our mother was different.

"Nice day you've got," remarked the wagon driver. "It was pouring cats and dogs yesterday. Grand weather for ducks it was."

Father cleared his throat and said, "It must be trying to arrive in a new land in pouring rain."

"You bet your boots, mister," the wagon driver laughed. "Where are youse bound for?"

"Upper Canada," my father told him, "Near a new town called Fergus in the township of Nichol. My brother and nephew are there now."

"The Queen's Bush, they call it," the driver answered, as if he knew the place like the back of his hand. "I've carted goods for many a family bound for those parts."

Nobody else said anything. Our silence went on and on, surrounded though we were by the bustling sights and sounds of the streets and squares we drove through. I did not dare speak. Purrkin's fate was still in doubt. If my mother put her foot down, even now, my cat would be handed over to the first cat-lover she could find. Afraid, all at once, that our friendly driver would express a longing for a kitten, I tried to hide him in a fold of my skirt.

Father began whistling "Flow Gently, Sweet Afton," but thought better of it after four or five bars. It was Hugh who broke the tension at last.

"That cat is my cat!" he said firmly, his eyes sparkling. "Hugh's."

Just as I opened my mouth to shout "No," Mother turned her head and gave me a daunting look.

"You can share him, Hugh," I gabbled. "But I'm the one who saved him so he's mostly mine."

Mother's bonnet hid her face again as she turned away. The taut silence started up again.

"I want a dog like old Shep," Charlie burst out, unable to stand more quiet.

"Me too," Hamish echoed too loudly. "Good ole Shep."

"At our new home, we already have a dog who's so like Shep he might be his twin," Father said. "He's waiting with your Uncle Thomas. He reminds me of you, Ailsa. He's stubborn and he's smart. Beautiful too."

Mother gave in then, with a sudden gasp of laughter.

"It's lucky that I'm partial to border collies," she said. "I was going to use the basket for victuals but I've changed my mind. Elspet, you may have it to keep your kitten in. That way, he might even arrive at our new home with all his whiskers. I'll give it to you when we get to the stage-coach office."

The wagon driver pulled on the reins and the old horse halted in front of an inn.

"Here you are, folks," he said. "Good luck to you wherever you end up. You've come to a grand place, you'll see."

Father gave him an extra sixpence for cheering us up. We scrambled down and looked around for our stage-coach. Not one was in sight. We had to wait again. Travelling seemed to be half moving along and half waiting to get started.

The people standing with us kept talking about all the immigrants who had died of cholera either on shipboard or soon after they arrived. Once my father said we were bound for Toronto, our fellow passengers looked us over from top to toe.

They seemed to stare at me especially hard. I did not understand it but it made me uncomfortable. Finally Mother spoke to them in a clipped voice.

"Our daughter does look a bit peaked but she is, I assure you, perfectly healthy. Her stomach gets upset when she's in a jouncing wagon, that's all."

Some of the travellers had the grace to flush and look away. But everyone seemed relieved too. I stared at them.

"Did they really think I might have cholera?" I whispered to my mother.

She nodded ever so slightly. I wanted to laugh but, instead, did my best to look hale and hearty. I knew I was thin and probably a bit green from the wagon ride but I thought they were foolish. Then, glancing at my parents' faces, I saw fear there too and bit back my laughter.

"I feel just fine," I declared in tones meant to reassure all who were interested.

Then I gazed down at Purrkin's sharp ears. Nothing terrible could be going to happen, not now I had my kitten.

The Lord would not bring us safely across that great dangerous ocean and then allow me to catch the cholera. I had that much trust in Providence.

"It'll be at least an hour more," a stable lad told Father.

"Then let's eat," Mother said. "We need not go into the inn. Who knows what pestilence might lurk indoors? Hamish, don't take up all the room on that stack of wood. Make a space for Charlie."

Hamish shifted obediently. Mother perched on the edge of the stone horse trough. Hugh and Purrkin and I settled on the grass at her feet. She turned to Father next.

"William, can you get us some cider? We need bread and cheese and maybe a piece of meat too. The thought of fresh meat makes my mouth water."

"Hamish, you'll have to come along. I'll need help to carry this banquet," my father said.

All our mouths were watering as we watched the door of the inn through which they had vanished. They came back, at last, laden with wonders. Father had a jug filled with cider, half a loaf of bread and a still hot pork pie. Hamish bore a half-dozen hardboiled eggs. He also had enough jam turnovers to go around. In no time, the boys were wolfing down slabs of pie, greedily licking the last drops of gravy off their fingers. I wanted to join in but could not put down my precious kitten.

Mother passed me the basket she had bought.

"Put him into it and eat your luncheon," she said.

"Thank you, Mother. Thank you, Father," I said in my sweetest voice. I loved them so much I would have hugged them if I hadn't had my cat in one hand and the basket in the other.

"I'll open the basket for you," Father said, seeing my predicament. "Now put him in. Good. Now wait, everyone, until we give thanks to the Lord for bringing us safely all this way."

The boys chewed fast, swallowed and pretended they had not started before we asked the blessing. Mother had a piece of cheese raised to her mouth but she put it down like a flash. We all bowed our heads obediently while Father prayed. We were thankful he, too, was hungry because it made him cut short his prayer.

Purrkin was surprised to be shut up but I dropped a bit of piecrust and a bite of bread in with him so he did not yowl even when I shut down the lid.

Happily munching my share of the feast, I thought of Furkin in Scotland. For the first time, I could picture Furkin curled up contentedly on Granny Ross's lap. They looked as peaceful as I felt, sitting in the sunshine in Montreal with Purrkin in his basket and fresh, tasty food in my hand.

At long last, the stage-coach rolled, rumbled and rattled in. The newly arrived passengers alighted and went into the inn to eat and drink. Fresh horses were harnessed up.

The coachman stood about gossiping with the men in the coach office. It was over two hours before we finally pulled out into the road.

How that coach jolted! The road was rough, and the farther we got from Montreal, the wilder the landscape seemed—and everywhere we looked, trees and more trees. The boys and Father got to ride up on top with the driver but my mother and Purrkin and I were cooped up inside. I soon felt sick again. Mother noticed my face turning greenish-white once more.

"Help me get this window open or she'll be ill," she told a stout farmer sitting opposite us.

The two of them wrestled open the window. In spite of the dust that came with it, fresh air helped my stomach to settle. Purrkin thought about vomiting but fell asleep instead. He was a smart kitten.

We stayed overnight in roadside inns. I found I was black-and-blue from the rough ride. I agreed with Charlie. Walking would be much better than this. There were bedbugs, too, and lice. Purrkin had fleas, of course. We were all half-mad with itching. Nobody said much about it. We were growing accustomed to bugs by now.

After many more weary miles, finally Father called down to us, "We'll be in Kingston in a few hours."

"Thank fortune!" Mother said. "To think I always longed to travel. Now I just want to sleep in the same bed two nights running."

We sailed up Lake Ontario in a steamboat. The lake looked as big as the ocean. Purrkin wanted out of his basket. He clawed at the lid and yowled. Finally I lifted it a little, meaning to pet him. He made himself thin as a streak and was gone faster than thought.

"Don't raise a rumpus," Father said testily. "If he doesn't know how to swim, we'll find him. He won't jump ship."

I wept harder than ever, shocked at how heartless my father could be. The entire family went searching.

"I got him!" Hamish said an hour later, in tones of deep disgust. But I knew he was as relieved as I was.

"Oh, Hamish, thank you," I said from my heart.

Finally we docked at Toronto, then a smaller town called Hamilton, late in the day.

"From here on, we mostly walk," Father said, sounding cheerful at the thought. He, like Charlie and me, had hated being bounced and banged along bad roads in the stage-coach.

Charlie and Hamish cheered.

"But not until morning," our father said. "We are going to sleep right here on the wharf tonight. There are no rooms to be had and we will run out of cash if we are not frugal. There won't be bedbugs out here."

There weren't. It was strange sleeping out on the wooden wharf under the stars. Some insects did dis-cover us and zipped in to suck our blood but we swatted them and, after a while, they seemed to give up.

"Are the stars here the same stars we see in Scotland?" I asked.

"Look and see," Father said with a yawn.

I gazed up into the starry sky and found familiar patterns one by one. The Big Dipper, Orion the Hunter, the Milky Way. Seeing them shining down so steadfastly was a great comfort. I drifted off, at last, curled up against my mother like a new lamb with its dam.

A shriek of laughter from Charlie woke me. Hamish had turned in his sleep and had roused to find his feet dangling into the lake. His boots and trouser legs were soaking. When he got up and tried to walk, his feet squelched.

"I guess you'll have to go barefoot," Father said.

The boys cheered again. I looked longingly at our parents.

"No, dear. Not you. Not Hugh either. The big boys will get blisters. Your soles aren't toughened up after weeks aboard ship. Wait and see," Mother said firmly.

We all walked much of the time from then on, passing first through pleasant farmland, then along ever-narrowing roads in wilder country. Our goods were brought along on an ox-cart pulled by two huge plodding creatures that sauntered more slowly than we did.

"They're regular slowtops," commented Hamish. "I can walk far faster."

The driver grinned down at him.

"They can walk much farther though, laddie," he said in

a slow fat voice. "The one is named Amble and the other is Meander. My wife named them. They never stop for a rest. They never get tuckered out or complain of blisters."

"Neither do I," Hamish said rashly.

But he did, just as Mother had said he would. Even though they hurt, he was proud of them. He and Charlie started up a contest to see which one could show the most and the biggest ones each time we stopped.

Father struck up a song when exhaustion slowed our steps. The music kept us marching briskly. It is surprising what a difference a song or rousing hymn can make.

"Guide us, O Thou Great Jehovah / Pilgrims in a weary land" came closest to saying how we really felt.

"When will we get there?" I asked for the hundredth time.

"Don't talk, walk," Father said in a clipped voice.

When I could not keep the tears from sliding down my cheeks, he reached out and relieved me of Purrkin's basket. I mopped my cheeks with my dusty sleeve and gave him a wobbly smile. I adored Purrkin but one small kitten and one middle-sized basket had grown so heavy I had been longing to dump them down and walk away. The boys had things to carry too. Father or Mother carried Hugh when he got really cranky. When he dozed off, the driver made a spot for him in the pile of luggage on the ox-cart.

We slept out, getting our clothes damp with dew. For once, being a girl was an advantage. Mother and I slept under the cart and were saved a wetting when a shower half drowned the others. The boys squeezed in around us but Father, gallantly, stayed drenched until morning.

It took us four days to make the better part of the journey to Nichol Township. I was trudging along, head down, doing my best not to bawl like a babe, when we came to a muddy track through what looked like dense forest.

"If we step lively, we'll be there for supper," Father told us. "Here's the trail we follow. It will lead us right to our own log house."

We stared at the rough path which wandered off into the forest. I was glad the trees had become less sinister. Seeing bluejays and sparrows, crows and finches flying in and out of their branches made me like them better. Watching a squirrel scamper up a tall trunk and dash along a limb until he jumped from branch to branch helped me forget my sore feet. I had never seen such bold, impudent animals in our glen.

"This little path? Here?" Charlie asked.

Father laughed. He did not sound tired any longer.

"Listen!" he told us. "That axe you hear may be Thomas chopping wood for our hearthfire."

"Let's go!" shouted Hamish, coming to life all at once. "Race you home, Charlie."

"I'm your man," Charlie shouted back.

And the two of them sprinted off as if they'd just wakened after a good night's sleep in a comfortable bed.

13

No Neighbours

"Boys, get back here," Father bellowed although he was laughing. "You may race but not with empty hands. Use your heads to save your heels."

The glum-faced boys came back. I stared at the path Father had indicated. It could only be seen for a few feet. Then it disappeared into the forest.

"Each of you big lads choose a box or bag to carry," Father said. "We only have a mile or so more to walk. I'll carry Hugh and Elspet will carry Purrkin. Thomas and Malcolm and I will come back for the rest of our goods. With Hamish and Charlie to help us, of course! Ailsa, don't look like that. It's better than it looks."

"I know," Mother said, her voice dragging with exhaustion. "Don't worry, William. I'll love it all—once I can sit down. I think I have several blisters myself. Big juicy blisters."

Both boys groaned. I, for once, was glad I was a girl. The driver of the ox-cart laughed and got out his pipe.

"I'll make sure no other traveller makes off with your possessions," he said comfortably.

Despite the loads they carried, the big boys raced ahead and then ran back, not wanting to lose their way. I lugged Purrkin but no longer noticed his weight, even though he had gained a lot since the day he found us. Finally, we made one last turning, went downhill for a bit and then looked through the trees. There before our eyes was a snug log cabin in a clearing and Uncle Thomas chopping wood in the dooryard. A dog so like Shep he made me blink bounded over to meet us. And Malcolm, fetching a bucket of water from a creek, dropped it and let out a whoop.

"Welcome home," shouted Uncle Thomas, jumping up and down as though he were Charlie. "Down, Laddie. Never mind the water, Malcolm. Hamish and Charlie will gladly fetch more, won't you, lads?"

"Welcome, Uncle William," Malcolm said, growing formal suddenly. "Welcome to Upper Canada, Aunt Ailsa."

"How about welcoming Cousin Hamish?" Hamish said.

"And Charlie and Hugh and Elspet Mary," Charlie added, laughing.

Malcolm sprang to cuff him, tripped on a root and tumbled head over heels, landing at Mother's feet.

"Haven't we met before, lassie?" he joked, grinning up at her.

Then, while we were all laughing, he jumped up and hugged her until she begged him to stop. What a lot of hugging there was! Everyone talked at once. The boys ran around exploring. I followed Mother up to the door and watched her lift the latch. Together the two of us entered our new home. Both of us recognized this was a solemn and important moment.

Inside it was much smaller than our cottage in Scotland. The main room, I learned later, was sixteen feet long and twelve feet wide. It had a rude fireplace with a chimney for the smoke to escape. There was a plank table with two benches, a big bed with a trundle tucked under it and a few rough shelves. Above it was a loft with a ladder leading up to it.

Later, I found an outbuilding, much smaller than the main cabin, built up against the rear wall. It held a pile of wood, a wooden bed frame, some tools and other jumble but it did not look finished.

I did not stop to look more carefully. Fascinating as it all was, I was not looking around yet. Instead I knelt by the hearth and opened the lid of Purrkin's basket.

"Don't run away, darling," I said to the big golden eyes glaring up at me. "This is your new home. Remember, you belong here …"

I should have remembered his getting lost on the ship and been careful to close the cabin door behind me. It stood open. Quicker than thought, Purrkin leapt out of the basket and vanished into the nearby small field of grain Uncle Thomas had cleared and sown. Was he going on into the densely crowding trees? I felt my heart break. It was all my own fault. He would be eaten by wolves or bears. Why hadn't I shut the door? If he never returned, it would be my doing. If he never returned …

"Don't look like that, my lamb. He'll be back," Mother said, sinking down on the stool next to the hearth where a fire had been lit in our honour. "Don't worry. As soon as I've got my wits about me, I'll get a saucer of food fixed for him."

"But that dog will eat him," I wailed, recollecting the leaping collie.

"Nonsense. Did Shep swallow Furkin? Laddie will ken at once that Purrkin is only a babe. I'm quite sure he won't harm a hair of his head," Mother said, adding a piece of birchwood to the dying fire and making it blaze up.

I scrubbed the tears off my face with my knuckles, leaving my cheeks streaked with grime, and I prayed for my cat to be cared for by the Lord who had brought us safely halfway around the world.

Then a roar of laughter sounded outside the door.

And into the cabin marched my proud Purrkin, a tiny mouse dangling from his small jaws. Right behind him came Laddie, deeply impressed, it was clear.

"Oh, you clever cat!" I cried.

Purrkin dropped the mouse as soon as we had seen it. He looked downright smug. He paid no attention when Mother picked up the mouse's limp body by its string of a tail and tossed it outside. Laddie ran to investigate but Purrkin remained by the cheery fire. Graciously he consented to eat a bit of moistened bread Mother had put on a tin plate.

"Can't he have cream?" I begged.

Father came in and answered before Mother could speak.

"We have to save the milk for you children. The calf needs a little too. Purrkin is used to scraps, remember. He will soon have rid us of the mice. They are a great nuisance."

Now that Purrkin had made himself at home, I ran to explore. I followed Hamish into the byre the men had built. A mild-eyed milk cow stood there with her young calf. They gazed at me without surprise. You would think we were old friends.

"Malcolm named the cow and calf," Hamish told me with a wicked grin. "The cow is Margaret and the calf is Molly."

I giggled. What would Granny Ross say to having a cow named after her? I doubted she would mind. She'd sniff, though. And Aunt Molly would look reproachful. Malcolm's mother was not nearly as ready to laugh as ours.

I went back out and looked around for other log houses and neighbours. Wherever I looked, all I saw were trees and underbrush. No hint of any other dwelling could be glimpsed. The trees around the clearing made a green wall which my glance could not penetrate.

"Where are the neighbours, Father?" I asked.

"No near neighbours yet, my girl. But one of these days they will come. And Thomas and I own two hundred acres. It is our own land. We are helping to build a new country in this wilderness. Think of that."

I forced myself to smile at him, remembering Granny's telling me not to mope. I even tried to be glad about it. It was nice, I supposed. But the tall dark trees, despite the birds and squirrels, made the place so different from the treeless land near Glen Buchan. I would never feel at home here. And I needed a girl to be my friend. Surely, somewhere in this new world of Father's, there must be such a girl!

14

The Rooster Crows

When we had finished moving everything indoors, the little log house was crammed to the rafters with people and their belongings. I was to sleep in the trundle bed beside Mother and Father's big bed. The boys would sleep on straw ticks in the loft. Uncle Thomas and Cousin Malcolm already had theirs up there. Charlie and Hamish jumped on the bulging straw-stuffed sacks which had been made ready for their coming, flattening them a little and filling the loft with choking dust.

"It's … making … me … sneeze!" yelled Charlie, suiting the action to the word.

"It will soon settle down and you won't notice," Malcolm said. "I'll sleep nearest the ladder so I can protect you from Hugh when he swarms up it and attacks us at dawn."

"You won't stay idling in your beds at dawn," Uncle Thomas said. "You'll pull on your shirts and britches and go milk Margaret."

I felt left out and lonely for a moment but I soon learned that there were plenty of jobs for girls. I often wished it were otherwise. Mother and I worked our fingers raw keeping our clothes and the cabin clean. We would just get the floor swept when one or other of the men or boys would tramp in with mud or even manure on his boots. Then it was all to do over. And we could not blame them. There seemed to be nowhere free of dirt. We washed clothes in the creek using homemade soap Father bought at market in Fergus.

"We'll make our own this fall," Mother said, eyeing the pig Uncle Thomas had brought home. He had built a shanty for another family and been given a piglet in payment.

"Do not become fond of that pig, Elspet," my father warned. "He's going to help feed us next winter. Do not give him a name or spend precious time scratching his back for him the way I saw you doing this morning."

After that, I avoided the pig pen whenever possible.

The cow Father had been so pleased to have waiting for us made plenty of work too. Not only did she have to be milked daily but we had to turn that milk into butter, buttermilk and cream. We set the milk to separate in big pans, skimmed off the cream when it rose and churned it to make butter and buttermilk.

We got meals ready for the men and boys, all of whom had stomachs like bottomless pits. We would make candles and soap after the pig was slaughtered. In the meantime, we used bought ones sparingly and went to bed early, so tired we were apt to be asleep before we had pulled our quilts up to our chins.

At first, Mother wished we had our own sheep so she could spin the wool and set up her loom but soon she admitted she was glad to let the making of cloth wait a year.

"I do not see how we could manage it," she said wearily.

We picked berries, crabapples, pin cherries and the plants she needed to make dye and medicine. We baked cornbread in an iron baking kettle. The bread was not the same as we had eaten in Scotland but it tasted good. All food tasted good when you worked as hard as we Gordons.

Most of these chores had had to be done in Scotland also but there Mother had had Granny to help her and, if the jobs were especially heavy, one of the village girls or her older sisters would lend a hand. In those days, with lots of hands making light work, I had been coddled, expected to help but never depended upon the way Mother did now. Now I was, of necessity, her right-hand girl and we both disliked it.

"I want some time to waste," I whispered. But I did not speak the thought aloud. When the boys or I complained about never having time to spend on our own pastimes, Mother reminded us how much better everything was than when we had been on shipboard and Father delivered his lecture on how good it was to own our own land and work for ourselves. We soon stopped grousing if either of them was within earshot. But I could tell I had Mother's secret sympathy as we looked at the filth trekked in on our scrubbed floor.

Finally my gentle mother grew short-tempered under the load of work. She never rested or ran out of chores for me to do. Father was bone-weary too. We could tell by the way he groaned getting to his feet after every meal. Uncle Thomas took to disappearing at odd times, claiming he was looking for a wife. We knew he was stretched out in the hay mow but did not tell. Even Malcolm's good humour wore thin as he did the work of a grown man.

In Glen Buchan, our parents had read aloud to us in the evening and had read to themselves too. Father still read the Bible aloud at mealtimes, of course, but now there was no time for any other reading. Although Father had unpacked the box of books first of all, they sat on the shelf and gathered dust for weeks. We had no time or energy now for *Pilgrim's Progress, The Poetry of Robert Burns* or the plays of William Shakespeare. All we still read regularly were the Old and New Testaments. I was glad there were good stories in there because I was hungry for tales of valour and romance.

"Mr. Dickens has written a new book," Father did say once. He had been to market and come home with news. "We can borrow it perhaps and read it this winter when we're snowbound."

In spite of chilblains and nowhere to go to get away from too many brothers, I could hardly wait for the luxury of being snowbound.

There was not a big crop that first summer but there was some wheat and lots of Indian corn. The land Father had bought had two apple trees close to the trail, which would become a road. One was a russet and one a yellow transparent. There was also a pear tree filled with bees and birds that liked the fruit as well as we did.

"How did those fruit trees get planted?" Mother wondered.

Father said that someone had tried homesteading here several years before but had lost heart and returned to the Old Country. They planted a few trees but left before there was any fruit. The wind helped some and so did animals, dropping apple and pear cores without eating every seed.

"We will not give up, William," Mother said grimly. "I could not face the ocean voyage again. Neither could Elspet."

I thought about Granny Ross so far away and Furkin on her knee. But I knew Mother was right. Gordons were never quitters.

"I need a girl to help with the work," my mother said one night. "There are five of you, not counting Hugh, to do the men's work here. But there are only Elspet and me to do all the jobs that are considered women's part. It is far too much for one woman and one nine-year-old, however hard we work. I had my mother and sisters to give me a hand in Glen Buchan and we could always get one of the MacTavishes in to lend a hand. But none of you men is of the least use."

My father looked ashamed of himself. He also looked worried.

"I ought to be shot not to have thought of it," he said. "I'll find you someone, Ailsa. She'll have to work for her bed and board and not much else, though. We haven't any money to spare."

"I know. Just do your best, Will," Mother said, giving him a smile.

"I still want neighbours," I muttered. "There are far too many boys and men. I need at least one girl."

Father laughed more happily at that.

"I'll see what I can do for you too," he said. "We want our women contented. Other settlers will come soon, I promise. Bide a wee while and you will see."

I longed to snap that I was sick and tired of biding a wee while but I heard Granny's voice inside my head saying, "Save your breath to cool your broth, my lass, and show respect for your elders and betters."

Father came home from Fergus two days later with a freckle-faced fourteen-year-old girl named Bridget. She talked a blue streak but she worked like a Trojan. I had a little more time to play but still no girl to play with me.

Then, after I had waited over a month, my invitation to meet the neighbours came at last. It happened in a way I would never have expected. Early that morning, Uncle Thomas and the boys went off to the nearest grist mill, leaving Father to get on with clearing some more of the land. Even Hugh went, promising faithfully to walk all the way home without whining if Uncle Thomas or Malcolm would let him ride on his shoulders on the way there. Mother and Bridget and I were busy when, suddenly, Father came rushing into the cabin.

Mother looked up from the churn. Bridget, on her way to fetch another bucket of water, stopped to stare. I quit peeling apples for sauce. We all waited to hear what had him so excited.

"Elspet, we have neighbours at last," he shouted at us as though we were a mile away. "Come on."

I sprang up, leaving the apples without a backward glance. Mother snorted and stayed where she was. The dasher went on thumping up and down inside the churn.

"Let Bridget past, Will," she said above the noise of the churning. "I didna hear anyone. I'll have butter in ten minutes if I don't stop. You go along, child. It's probably a doe and fawn or some such creatures. If there's need for me to come, run back and fetch me. But recollect that Bridget and I have no spare time this morning. She's leaving after we finish the chores to go see her mother."

"But, Ailsa ..." Father started.

She did not let him finish.

"I've seen enough fascinating Canadian wildlife to last me a fortnight. Now I have work to do. Bridget, if you want to visit your mother, you'd better not stand about with your mouth open."

My father gave Mother a wry look. He stood back and let Bridget sidle past. Then he led me out the door. Sure enough, when I stood on the step and looked about, nobody was in the clearing. I didn't even see a deer browsing or another kind of woodpecker.

Father could get very excited about a new kind of bird. He had made us stand for ages watching a tall blue heron fishing in Cox's Creek and a chipmunk stuffing his cheeks with nuts. Mother usually was interested too, but she had lost some of her curiosity lately. She said her back ached.

"Where are the neighbours?" I demanded suspiciously.

"Hark and you'll hear," my father said.

I was delighted that I was sharing these moments with my father without a brother shoving his oar in. I trotted after him ready for anything but not too hopeful.

"I don't hear ...," I started to say.

Then I did hear it. A rooster was crowing!

"Nobody within earshot has hens. These must be new people and they can't be that far away," Father said, looking mightily pleased with himself. "Wait right there. I'll get some bread and cheese. We can stay out of your mother's hair without worrying about our dinner getting cold."

He was back in a moment with a packet of food shoved into his wide pocket. He also had my boots. He grinned at me like a boy playing truant from school.

"Put these on or you'll stub your tender toes," he said.

I pulled them on as fast as I could.

"Come on," he said, picking up an axe and striding toward a gap in the trees. "There's a deer trail we can follow on the other side of this fallen log. Give me your hand, lassie. Now jump. When the trees grow too close, I'll blaze a trail so we won't get lost coming back."

His plan sounded simple. It was not simple to put into action, though. The deer trail might have been easy for a deer. It was terribly difficult for a girl in a long, full skirt. Yet, even though branches swung back and slapped me in the face and flies nipped and nibbled at our ears and foreheads, we made steady headway. Every time we did grow discouraged, the helpful rooster sang out again as though he knew we were coming and he was determined to guide us all the way.

I was too excited to mind a few scratches. I tore a leafy switch from a sapling we passed and swung it back and forth around my head and shoulders. I was glad I had snatched up my sunbonnet from the hook by the door. It kept some of the insects off.

I had rarely been alone with my father for such a long time. We had had few chances to share in expeditions like this. Hamish was usually the chosen one. Yet here Father and I were, making a voyage of discovery together. I felt like Balboa or Sir Francis Drake.

After an hour, we stumbled into a natural clearing with a big shelving rock. It looked like a flattish limestone couch. A few feet from it, Father uncovered a spring almost hidden by grass and leaves. The two of us cleaned it out and drank thirstily. Then Father pulled out the package of bread and cheese.

"We need fortifying, wouldn't you say?" he said with a grin.

We sat, side by side, and ate every last crumb. Afterwards, we finished off with another long drink of spring water.

"Your mother will be sorry she missed this," my father told me, "but she can come later. When we visit back and forth, this spring and rock seat will make a perfect resting spot. You and I will find these people with a rooster all by ourselves, this first time, but we'll probably do lots of travelling to and fro."

I did not care about the future. The rooster crowed more lustily than ever.

"Lead on, Macduff," I said, quoting one of his favourite sayings.

He laughed and set out ahead of me. We speeded up a little. We found the second part of the journey harder because the deer trail branched off, leading away from the rooster's inviting crow. We hacked a path through prickly bushes and clambered over more fallen logs. I put my foot on one and my boot sank into a rotten bit and made me slip. Father caught my flailing arm, though, and we kept going. I stumbled again and fell but I scrambled up before he had to come to my rescue. I wanted him to see that I was every bit as tough as Hamish or Charlie. I was thankful we had stopped to eat. I could tell by the sunlight sifting down through the leaves that our usual dinner hour was long past.

Father cut blazes in the trees as we went. Then, all of a sudden, to our astonishment, we broke through one last clump of trees and stepped into a fair-sized clearing surrounded by stumps. Getting rid of the stumps was back-breaking work. They stood about everywhere like rotting wooden teeth.

But I had no attention to spare for tree stumps. As I staggered into the sunny space, the first person I saw was a girl my own age sitting on the step of a log shanty, smaller and more rickety than our own. She had black braids that curled at the ends. She was barefoot. She wore a faded pink sunbonnet and a dull brown homespun dress very like my own. She was watching the bush a little nervously and, on her lap, was a skinny calico cat.

15

Jeanie Mackay

I usually can't think what to say when I meet someone new. But this time, I did not wait for Father to speak first. Words burst out of me like water gushing from a fountain.

"We heard your rooster," I babbled, my cheeks flushing with delight. "We came to find you. I'm Elspet Mary Gordon. What's your name? When did you come here? And what do you call your cat?"

The girl stood up. The calico cat sprang to the ground and stalked off in a huff. But it did not go far.

"We've been here two weeks but Pa just brought the rooster yesterday. My cat's called Motley. I'm Jeanie

Mackay," the girl said. "Mother!"

The door behind her opened while she was turning to push it wide. A roundish woman, with hair as glossy black as the girl's, stepped out. She stared at Father and me as though we were ghosts. Her eyes were wide with surprise. Then she remembered her manners and came forward.

"Good day," she said a little stiffly. "I'm Mrs. Robert Mackay. You are the first people I've laid eyes on since we arrived in this wilderness. My daughter and I have just been here ten days."

The cat watched from a nearby stump, her tail twitching. Jeanie smiled at me. She was shy too, I could tell, but her smile was friendly. Maybe she, also, had been longing for another girl to talk to.

"We're two of the Gordon clan," Father said. He shook Mrs. Mackay's hand warmly. "I'm William and this is Elspet Mary. We call her Elspet mostly. We blazed a trail through the bush when we heard your rooster. His crow told me that at last we had near neighbours. I can't understand why we didn't hear you building your shanty. My Elspet is overjoyed. She has been longing for a girl her age ever since we arrived late in July."

Jeanie laughed aloud. Mrs. Mackay's smile grew a tiny bit warmer.

"It's always good to have neighbours," she said, "especially when you are so far from home."

It didn't take that long to get here, I thought, and then realized that, when she said "far from home," she was speaking of Scotland. Was our log cabin "home" to me then? I did not know.

"We have three boys at home but only one girl," Father went on, grinning at Jeanie. "My wife Ailsa would have come too if she hadn't been in the middle of churning."

"We have only the one child now," Jeanie's mother said. Her smile went out like a candle flame being snuffed. Her voice was low and full of pain. "We stayed at an inn in Montreal, never guessing cholera had already broken out there. Our Alastair was sickly after the voyage and, when he caught the foul disease in Montreal, he had no' the strength to fight it off. He was just a wee bairn ..."

At this, her voice broke and her eyes filled with tears. I looked away. Jeanie squeezed her mother's hand.

"Don't forget Jamie," she said softly. "We have Jamie, Mam."

"No, I'm not forgetting him," her mother said. Her words grated harshly and sounded lifeless. "But he's none of mine."

"He is ours now!" the little girl insisted, her eyes fierce and her chin high. "I'll get him. He's waking up. They'll want to meet him."

Her mother shot her an annoyed glance but Jeanie vanished into the cabin. I stood mutely listening to Father and Mrs. Mackay talking. They sounded like people in church. She was explaining something about Mr. Mackay's having come to Upper Canada first and bought the land while she and the children waited in Montreal. He had found this place with a shanty already erected. The people who had built it had no title to the land and had been glad to be bought off with a few pounds.

"My husband is no builder," she said in a cold voice.

That's why we did not hear the axe chopping or the hammer driving in nails, I thought.

I looked over at Father for permission to go after Jeanie. When he nodded, I followed her inside. She was bending over a cot. In it lay the homeliest baby I had ever seen. His hair stood up in a bush of bouncy red curls. His eyes were brilliant blue. His little ears stuck out like cup handles. He had a wide mouth and a nub of a nose.

Just looking at his funny face made me laugh aloud. Jeanie scowled at me.

"He's beautiful, isn't he?" she said defiantly.

"Beautiful," I said quickly, doing my best not to laugh again. I knew how I would feel if Jeanie Mackay made fun of our Hugh. But did Jeanie really believe Jamie was beautiful? How could she? She must be just saying so because she loved him.

Jeanie picked the grinning baby up and held him tight.

"When we were waiting for Pa, Jamie's family was staying in the same inn. The cholera killed all of them except Jamie," she muttered, her eyes on the door. "Our Alastair sickened too and, in just a few hours, he was gone."

I gasped and stared at her white face as she went doggedly on.

"When my Pa came, I was looking after wee Jamie and Ma was sore grieving. So my father said God must mean us to take the poor orphan with us, since he needed us and we needed him. I was glad. But Mam still thinks only of Alastair. She says we must find Jamie's folks. Pa did ask about them. Nobody knew who they were. We could keep him if she'd a mind to do so. But she wants him gone."

I looked at the cheerful little boy and felt a tightness inside my chest. He was an orphan like me. He was laughing. He did not seem to mind being an orphan. But he was too little to understand that Mrs. Mackay did not want him.

My family had wanted me. I was sure of that. They had never once said, "She's none of ours."

Or had they? Grandfather Gordon had said just that.

The rooster crowed again. Jeanie looked up from Jamie's funny face. She smiled at me. The smile made her eyes light up.

"I'm so glad our rooster found you," she said. "Mam is so sad. I needed a friend."

I smiled back at her. She still looked very lonely despite the bright smile. She was missing Alastair and scared of losing Jamie too. She wanted him with all her heart. What could I say?

"We didn't adopt a baby here," I said, trying to help in the only way I could think of. "We adopted a kitten. We got him in Montreal. What did you say your cat's name is?"

"Miss Motley," Jeanie said. "She wears motley clothes like a jester. We found her near here. She was starving and lost."

"Just like Purrkin," I said.

We sat down for a moment and went on talking. I told her all about Purrkin's flying through the air and landing right at my feet.

"Is your mother wanting to get rid of Motley too?" I asked.

Jeanie made a face.

"Not she. She hates mice. As long as Motley is a good mouser, she'll have a home with us. She left four dead ones on the doorstep this morning."

"Why don't you come back with us and meet Mother?" I said as we started to go out again. "It's a long way through the bush but part of it is a deer track. Mother will want to meet your mother. And I want you to see Purrkin."

"I canna," Jeanie said at once. She held the baby close. "I have to bide wi' Mam and Jamie. She willna leave this clearing. I mun ..."

She stopped. She looked as though she would love to come.

"We could bring Mother here," I said doubtfully. She would have finished the churning but I knew she would have started on some other work. She might be peeling the rest of the apples. "She knows what to do for sad people. She had two children who died. She might be able to help your mother. I'll ask Father."

We went back outside. Jeanie carried Jamie in her arms. I blinked at the sudden light. Inside the Mackays' shanty it had been very dark. Mrs. Mackay saw the baby in her daughter's arms. But her eyes stayed cold and sad. She did not look at him as Mother looked at Hugh. She glanced away at once, as though the very sight of the little boy galled her.

"He was awake," Jeanie said quickly. "Isn't he a lovely bairn, Mr. Gordon?"

Her mother gave a scornful snort but Father seemed not to hear it. He grinned at Jamie and Jamie grinned back. Watching them, I could not help but chuckle.

"He's certainly a happy wee chap," my father said. "Come see me, my braw laddie."

Jamie put out his arms and went to Father exactly the way Hugh did. I puzzled over this instant trust. How did babies always know Father loved them? They all knew. Well, I, too, had known he was to be trusted on the night Da brought me from Aberdeen. It had something to do with his quiet eyes.

"Leave a note for your husband, Mrs. Mackay," Father said then. "I'd like to take you to meet the rest of our family."

Mrs. Mackay's face went rock-hard.

"Not today," she said flatly.

"I'll write the note," he said, his tone gentle.

"No," Mrs. Mackay repeated, her cheeks as red as fire now.

Before Father could persuade her to change her mind, Jeanie's Pa came out of the bush. He had a heavy sack on his back. He slid it to the ground and stared at Father and me in astonishment.

"Where did you two spring from?" he asked.

"We heard your rooster crow," Father said smoothly. "So my daughter and I came to find our neighbours. I was going to write you a note to say I'd taken your wife to meet mine. I'm William Gordon and this is my Elspet."

Mr. Mackay's cheeks also reddened but he stretched out his hand to shake Father's.

"My wife does the reading in our house," Jeanie's father said. "I can write my name and work with figures a bit. But I can't read."

I was shocked but Father did not so much as blink. Father had loved books since he was a boy in school and had wanted to go on to grammar school but Grandfather Gordon saw no sense in book learning beyond a certain point. I knew that half the older people in the glen could not read. Charlie was not much of a reader even though Mother insisted that he keep working at his lessons in the winter. I already read better than Charlie.

"That doesn't matter," Father insisted, not meeting Mrs. Mackay's eyes. "My wife needs a neighbour to talk to. Come on, all of you. I'll lead the way and carry this lump of a lad."

Jamie chortled and pulled my father's hair.

"Easy does it, my young friend," Father told him and turned back to the opening in the bush through which we had come. He did not wait for the Mackays' approval but walked confidently into the trees. Jeanie and I glanced sideways at each other. We stood poised, ready to go either way. A full minute crawled by. Then Mr. Mackay lugged the sack inside the shanty. When he emerged, without saying a word to us, he and his wife followed Father and Jamie. We dashed after them, wild with suppressed elation.

"Your father is like ... like a laird," Jeanie whispered.

Although I knew he was not a bit like the laird in the great house near our glen, I understood what she meant and I felt proud of him.

Out of the corner of my eye, I saw Miss Motley come after us. She darted forward, pouncing ahead and peering back. I didn't draw Jeanie's attention to her. Why shouldn't a cat come to meet the neighbours too? Purrkin might be pining for cat company.

16

Changeling

Despite there being so many more of us, it took much less time going home. Father and I had broken off branches and bent others back out of the way. Father's axe had cut through other brambly bits. I explained that it would be even easier when we reached the deer track, and this encouraged Jeanie. She repeated the news in a voice loud enough to reach her parents' ears. All the same, our feet were starting to drag when we came to the rock couch and little spring.

"We rest here," I told my new friend importantly, as though I had done so countless times. We knelt by the bubbling spring. Cupping our hands, we drank thirstily.

"We'll catch our breath for a bit," my father said. "Here come your parents now."

The Mackays were silent as they reached the resting rock. Mrs. Mackay still looked angry. Jeanie's father's mouth was shut tight. Jeanie went quickly to take her mother's hand again. Even that loving touch did not make Mrs. Mackay's face soften.

"Sit down and rest," Father said as though he noticed nothing out of the way. "We can go on when we're refreshed."

He set Jamie down on the grass by Jeanie and me. Then he got out his knife and cut a piece of birch bark. Deftly, he shaped the strip into a cone.

"Here's a backwoods drinking cup," he told them. "Take it, man, get your woman a sip of cold spring water. She looks as though she needs it. I'll make another for the laddie."

The back of Mr. Mackay's neck was brick-red as he stooped to fill the little cup at the spring. He bore it to his wife. It leaked badly which made us laugh. Mrs. Mackay caught her husband's eye and smiled in spite of herself. She drank gratefully and held out the cup for more. Jamie put his nose right into the cone Father held to his lips and drank noisily.

When we all rose to go, the mood was happier. Father had picked Jamie up but, when Mr. Mackay reached out for him, Father handed the baby over without a word. He flexed his arm as though Jamie had weighed a ton.

"You're feeding him well," he said.

"He shan't starve while he's in my care," Mrs. Mackay snapped, her eyes going dull again. "They shan't say I didn't look after him well. I do my duty by him, for all it means extra work."

Father glanced at her but did not respond to what she had said.

"You girls run ahead. Tell your mother we're coming, Elspet," Father said calmly. "It's clear enough most of the way now."

I, with Jeanie at my heels, tore ahead, crashing through any underbrush that threatened to slow me down. I was glad to get away from Mrs. Mackay's set face and wounding words. Jeanie seemed to share my relief although she glanced back every so often.

"Mother!" I called as we reached our own clearing. "Mother, we found neighbours."

Mother, drying her wet hands on her sack apron, came to the cabin door. She smiled a warm welcome as she caught sight of Jeanie.

"This is Jeanie Mackay," I said, my words tumbling out in an excited rush. "Her mother and father are coming behind us. We found them by following the crowing of their rooster. They have a baby …"

Mother was turning to put the kettle on. Then something in my face and tone made her pause. She gave Jeanie a searching look.

"Elspet has a baby brother too," she told her. "But Hugh's turning into a boy as fast as he can. How old is your little brother, child?"

Jeanie hesitated.

"We think he's about ten months," she said at last. "My mother ... We lost our own baby Alastair. Cholera broke out in the inn where we were staying in Montreal. My mother's sair grievin'."

"Here they come," I broke in, guessing Mrs. Mackay would not be pleased to catch Jeanie telling all their secrets. "He's the funniest baby."

"He's lovely," Jeanie muttered, staring at the group entering the clearing. "His name is Jamie."

Mother didn't go inside after all. She went quickly to meet Mrs. Mackay. Without paying any attention to the shut look on the other woman's face, she put her arms around her.

"You've had a sad time of it, my dear," I heard her say softly. "Come on in and lay your burden down for a bit."

Mrs. Mackay let Mother lead her into the cabin. At the door, Mother turned and looked at Father.

"Bridget's mother is ill. I told her she needn't come back until morning. I'll call you when we want you," she said. Then she shut the door.

"Give me Jamie," Jeanie said to her father. "You go with Mr. Gordon. I'll tend him."

I looked at her in surprise. She sounded like an adult. Her father handed the baby over. He and Father walked off together. I caught enough of their conversation to know they were discussing what their lives had been in Scotland and what their problems were here in Upper Canada. Part of me wanted to tag along after them and listen. I liked listening to adult talk. But the boys would be back before long. I had no time to waste. I hoped Uncle Thomas would take his time chatting with the miller.

"Come over here," I told my new friend. "We can sit on the bench."

We sat side by side and did not know how to begin. Then Jeanie burst out, "Do you miss your old home?"

"Yes," I said at once. I spoke quietly. I did not want Mother or Father to hear. But it was wonderful to be able to speak the truth without getting a lecture on how fine this new land was. "I miss Granny Ross. I miss my cat Furkin, too, and all the people at home. I even miss the burn behind our cottage and the heather … but not as much as I did at first. I had a friend called Maggie MacTavish. Her family went to Nova Scotia. I haven't had anyone but boys or adults to talk with since … until this minute."

"I miss Alastair," Jeanie told me. She spoke softly too.

"How old was he?"

"Older than Jamie. Nearly two. He was so loving … It was terrible at the inn. Alastair begged for fresh buttermilk.

He thought he was at home. We had none to give him and he kept crying. Then he stopped and I wished he would start again. And now Mam is not like herself. It's as though she is under a spell."

Jeanie looked frightened as soon as the words were out. Then, inside the cabin, Mrs. Mackay cried aloud, "He's none of mine. I won't have an ugly little changeling in my Alastair's place!"

"Hush, hush," Mother said, the way she did when Hugh skinned his knee and she was comforting him.

"Oh, my poor laddie! How could the Lord God take an innocent child in that cruel way? I won't keep the other. I won't!"

The bitter words came clearly through the chinks in the wall. I froze. I stared at Jeanie in horror. Had she told me this? I supposed she had. But I had not be-lieved it for a moment. I had not understood that Mrs. Mackay intended to give Jeanie's beloved "beautiful" baby away. Yet my friend's eyes were dark with misery, not wide with surprise.

"She can't really mean it," I breathed.

"She doesn't want him," Jeanie said woodenly, reaching to touch Jamie's springy hair. "Father hoped he would ease her but she says we canna keep him. I told you already but you did not take it in. I know he's not Alastair. Alastair was so bonny and wee Jamie is not that way. I ken that much. It hurts her to see his funny face. But, oh, Elspet, I do love him so. He eases the hurt for Father too."

I had no notion what to say to her. I knew about changelings, of course. Granny Ross told stories about them. The heartless fairies stole the human baby and put a changeling in its place. But Jamie was not one of those ugly little fairy creatures. He might look like an imp but he was a real human child. Jeanie would never love a changeling the way she loved wee Jamie.

Mrs. Mackay was crying more quietly now.

"You canna not keep him," I whispered. "It's not his fault his parents died. You are the only family he has now."

In my memory, Mother's voice was saying, "Of course we'll keep her. She belongs with us. We're her family."

Yet Mother had lost Fiona and Robbie. Fiona had been two. Had Mother felt …? What if she had said, "She's none of mine." Where would I have gone then?

"Do you think he knows?" I whispered, unable to bear the hurt I felt for the orphan Jamie.

"No," Jeanie murmured. "I try not to let him hear. And she is kind to him, Elspet … I keep hoping something will happen to change her mind."

Then Purrkin came strolling out from behind the cabin and Miss Motley walked daintily out of the bush.

"Oh, Motley!" Jeanie cried, pushing all thought of her mother aside for a moment. "How did you get here?"

"Purrkin, behave." I started up, reaching for him.

But the two cats ignored both of us. They were still kittens really and they, too, had been wanting someone to play with. They sprang at each other, jumped back, batted their paws in the air, dodged sideways and rushed forward again. It was like a dance almost. Jamie laughed uproariously and tried to grab Purrkin's tail as he went leaping past. Purrkin was gone, though. He and Motley were wrestling. Soon Jeanie and I were laughing helplessly.

Then, just as I recollected Mrs. Mackay calling wee Jamie a changeling, Uncle Thomas, Malcolm and my brothers filed up the path. All five of them carried loads. Even Hugh was lugging a fat squash. The others bore sacks of corn meal, a sharpened scythe blade, potatoes and a bag of smaller goods.

I turned to call Mother but she opened the cabin door.

"Elspet Mary, lend a hand," she commanded. Then, turning to Mrs. Mackay, she said, "You must stay and eat with us."

"Not tonight," Jeanie's mother said. "We left without doing our chores. And the daylight is so soon over now."

There was no more quiet after that. The Mackays set out, Mr. Mackay carrying Jamie once more. He smiled gratefully at my mother as he settled the baby into the crook of his arm.

"Thank you, Mrs. Gordon," he said. "She needs another woman badly."

"We all need each other," Mother said. "Say a word of thanks to that rooster. Elspet and I especially were pining for neighbours."

Then the Mackays and little Jamie disappeared down the trail Father had blazed earlier.

The boys ran off to do their chores. Mother stood looking at the spot in the trees where the Mackays had vanished.

"Changeling indeed!" I heard her mutter.

Then she turned and went back inside. She shut the door with a decided bang. I was glad. I had not liked Mrs. Mackay's bitter words either. "Purrkin, we have neighbours now," I said, picking up my kitten who, by now, was almost roly-poly.

Purrkin purred in a highly satisfactory rumble.

"Their baby isn't a changeling," I whispered into the cat's soft fur. "He's a darling. And he belongs here."

17

None of Mine

Late that night, I wakened with a start. Still caught in a frightful dream, I made not a sound. The faceless man who had haunted my dreams before had come for me again. But this time, I had seen who he was. Grandfather Gordon. In the dream I had been running at full stretch, when Father had poked the fire. A log split with a crack and woke me. I gave a sigh of relief. I was safe.

I did not call out to my mother. Since I slept in the trundle bed near their large one, I could see and hear them from the moment my eyes opened. I was, after all, nine and no longer a baby. Also, I liked watching them without their noticing me. I half closed my eyes and lay peeking through my lashes. Mother bent over the table and blew out the lamp. They were coming to bed. It must be very late.

Although there was no lamplight now, I could still see them moving about. Moonlight streamed through the window's one glazed pane. There was also a flickering light from the hearth. It was cosy.

I listened to the comforting noises they made, banking the fire, talking softly, putting things away, undressing. I loved pretending to be asleep while they talked. But this time, I strained my ears. I needed to hear Mother say I was still her own girl. I knew, from experience, that they were more likely to talk about the corn crop or what sort of hens to buy. But I kept hoping to catch the sound of my own name.

Maybe it was the dream. Maybe it was hearing about Jamie. Whatever it was, I longed for them to say, clearly and without doubt, that I belonged to them, that they felt toward me exactly what they would feel if I had been born to them in the usual way.

Hugh, tucked up in his cot, snored softly through his open mouth. I strained my ears. At last, Mother spoke.

"That poor woman!" she said. "Losing her boy like that must have been dreadful. It's too bad Mr. Mackay didn't wait a bit longer before he decided they should take in young Jamie."

"He's a homely little chap, isn't he?" Father said, yawning and laughing at the same time. "Did you see his comical grin, Ailsa? I almost whooped with laughter. And their Jeanie kept staring straight at me, sober as a judge, and asking me if I didn't think he was beautiful. He doesn't resemble them at all."

"He's a dear," Mother said sharply. "I feel for Janet Mackay but she's too wrapped up in herself. It hasn't crossed her mind that her husband and her little girl are grieving too. She acts as though the boy who died was hers and hers alone. Yet Mr. Mackay and Jeanie are suffering greatly. They need that baby. Jamie must miss his mother, for that matter."

Father pulled off his boots. The bed creaked as he stretched out on it with a gusty sigh.

"Beds are miraculous things," he said. "There's nothing quite so healing to aches and pains as sleeping in a real bed."

I grinned but Mother ignored his idle words.

"I almost told her about Elspet," she murmured. "I will tell her when it's time. I know how it is for the poor woman. How desperate I felt when Fiona and Robbie were taken from me! I was sure I'd never smile again."

"You wanted Elspet, though, the moment Rolf put her into your arms," Father said. He sounded wide awake now. "I remember your holding her and saying she could bide."

"Of course," Mother said, laughing softly as she, too, remembered. "She looked up at me with your eyes and she needed a mother so. I was won over before I had time to think."

"Kirsty's eyes, you mean."

"Your eyes too," my mother told him. "You both had those eyes. You know I loved her from the moment I took her, as you say. But I'd had four months to start healing, William. It sounds to me as though Mrs. Mackay had no time at all."

"The bairn's family probably died when the Mackays' boy did. The poor man had no choice," Father defended Jeanie's Pa.

"Kirsty was your sister but, when Rolf brought Elspet to us, you didn't push me …"

"You needed no push, my love," he said, yawning again. "I couldn't have wrested her from you if I had wanted to. Tell Mrs. Mackay if you must. But be careful. Elspet must not be hurt. She's forgotten being brought to us so long ago. I doubt she even remembers her father. She cannot recall Kirsty."

"I think she does remember. Elspet Mary keeps her secrets. I'll take care, William. But that woman must be brought to her senses or there will be more tragedy in that family. Her own heart will break if she lets that imp be taken from her."

"Maybe she'll come around on her own …"

"Not she. She's like your father. She's made her stand and she's a stubborn Scot. She may well stick to her guns while her world falls to pieces around her."

There was a long moment of silence. I thought Father was asleep. Then he roused himself.

"Well, Ailsa, you're an expert at mending broken hearts," he mumbled. He was sounding sleepier every minute.

"I will speak to Elspet. The time has come for it, in any case," Mother said under her breath. She seemed to be talking to herself now.

I waited for Father to answer. He started to snore instead. Soon both of them were breathing deeply. I lay wakeful, thinking over what I had heard. They had wanted me.

Then I was back there once more, a little girl bundled up in her father's plaid, being given into Mother's warm arms. She thought now that she had loved me always. But had she wanted me that night? In her heart of hearts, had she hesitated for a few seconds? Had my Da made her give me a home? Had she agreed only because there was nobody else?

The sickening questions struck at me like hammer blows. I felt a coldness creeping through me as I struggled to remember. Mother had held me close. I myself had felt so utterly safe. Yet had Mother secretly wanted Da to take me away? If he had ridden to Grandfather Gordon's big house, would they have said, "She's none of ours. She doesn't resemble us in any way."

Granny Ross had often talked to me about my Mam.

"Pretty as a picture she was but no better than she should be. Always wanting to get away from the village and have a fine life in some city. And look where it got her!"

That was what she had said. Or had I gotten it mixed up? Purrkin pushed his whiskery face under my chin but I hardly noticed. He washed my nose with his hot raspy tongue. At last, I put my hand up and stroked his sleek fur but I was still not really thinking about him.

Changeling, I was thinking. And I heard again, inside my head, Mrs. Mackay crying out the terrible words, "He's none of mine."

Maybe, just maybe, my family had taken me in because it was their duty. Maybe, just maybe, they secretly agreed with Grandmother Gordon when she said, "She isn't a bit like us."

18

Heart of My Heart

Next morning, I did not want to get out of bed.

"Come along, slugabed," my mother said at last, twitching off my warm quilts. "We have work to do."

Bridget had come back just after sun-up. The three of us worked hard all morning making candles. I hated the job. I kept my eyes lowered, unable to look right at my mother. I felt weary and lost.

"What's the matter, Elsie? Did you get out of bed on the wrong side this morning?" Bridget teased.

"Don't call me Elsie," I muttered.

Bridget laughed. I longed to smack her silly face but kept

silent and went on working. Mother did not seem to notice my dismal mood.

The boys clattered in and out. Hamish brought in the milk pails. Charlie split kindling for the fire and carried it to the woodbox. Hugh, his tongue attached in the middle and wagging at both ends, was constantly underfoot and as noisy as the squirrels that scolded us all from nearby trees.

My mother and Bridget chatted. Bridget had picked up lots of gossip while visiting her family. The only thing she said that caught my interest was the news that they were planning to build a library in Ennotville. I longed to know more but I did not let myself ask.

Then, late in the morning, Mr. Mackay brought the children over.

"My wife is feeling poorly," he said, his eyes anxious. "If you could find time to look after our two for the day, you'd be doing her a great kindness. She still has not recovered from the rigours of the journey. I have almost given up trying to get her to accept the little lad. She seems to have set her mind against keeping him. Tomorrow I suppose I must start to search for another family for him."

"Of course I can keep them here," Mother said. Then she laughed. "It will fit in perfectly with a scheme of my own. I'm sorry she's ill but I'm happy to have the children. Take Bridget back with you. She's a good practical girl. She can cosset your wife a bit and, later on, I'll see the children get home."

"Thank you," Mr. Mackay said simply.

Bridget practically skipped across the clearing. Caring for one sick lady was a grand rest from helping cook and clean up after all of us Gordons.

Jeanie and I worked in the garden patch. Some of my grey misery lifted a little as we weeded. It was much easier working with somebody to share the tasks. We helped prepare the noon meal. Mother sent us to the creek to look for cress and we paddled our bare feet in the cold water. I stopped feeling like Purrkin with his fur rubbed the wrong way.

Late in the afternoon, Mother called Jeanie.

"It's time you were getting home," she said with a smile. "Your mother may want you to take care of her. Hamish will walk through the bush with you and bring Bridget home. He'll keep all the wild beasts at bay. I have a note for you to give to your mother."

Jeanie reached for Jamie but my mother stopped her. "I'll keep him here with me for a bit," she said, her tone light, her eyes sparkling. "Don't worry, child. I've explained everything in the letter. You run along. But see to it that she reads my note the minute you get home."

Jeanie looked uncertain. But Mother was so firm. At last, Jeanie kissed Jamie and started walking into the woods. Hamish swaggered at her side, pleased to be trusted to protect her. Mother made sure he carried a stout stick.

"Why did you keep Jamie here?" I asked when they were out of hearing.

Mother gave Jamie some spools to play with. Then she sat down and drew me to her.

"I have a scheme," she said, "and I want to tell you a story. You knew it once but I must be very sure you have not lost track of it."

I thought of pulling away. I could not make myself do it. All day, I had been longing to lean my head against her and feel her arms close around me. I already guessed that the story would change everything back to the way it had been. I so wanted to be my mother's own Elspet Mary again. I yearned to return to being the cherished child I had been ever since Da gave me into her arms.

"Once upon a time, there was a boy called William. He had three brothers and one little sister named Kirsty. When they were children, he and Kirsty were thick as thieves," Mother said. "When they grew up, Kirsty was lovely to look at. She was so bonny her parents were afraid for her and they tried to keep her safe. They caged her in with rules and preached fire-and-brimstone sermons at her. Naturally young Kirsty longed to fly free. Then a fair-haired, good-hearted seaman came to the glen. He fell in love with the beautiful girl and asked to marry her."

"Did you see him?" I broke in, all agog at the turn her tale was taking.

"I did," Mother said. "I thought he was wonderful too. But he had eyes only for Kirsty. Her parents were afraid of losing their lovely daughter so they forbade her to see him again."

I stirred uneasily. Mother waited for me to listen once more. When I was still, she went on.

"Kirsty could not bear losing Rolf. She ran off with him instead," she said, her voice tinged with sadness. "She was only fifteen. Everyone missed her sorely. Nobody knew where she had gone. Her family was frantic with worry."

"That was unkind of her," I said, wishing my mother would be as kind as she was beautiful.

"A little unkind," my mother agreed. "But, if she had refused to see Rolf ever again, I would never have met you, my honey. Hush now while I tell you the rest. Rolf and Kirsty had a baby girl and christened her Elspet Mary. Kirsty wrote to us and told us about that baby. Then Rolf had to go back to sea and Kirsty was killed in a street accident. Kind neighbours took in little Elspet Mary until her father came home from the sea. When he learned that his Kirsty was lost to him, he took his little girl to Kirsty's brother William and his wife Ailsa and asked them to care for her."

Mother stopped for an instant. Then she went steadily on.

"Granny Gordon would have kept you, I think, but your father would not leave you in that house. I would not have let you go anyway, heart of my heart. From the moment you got your little hands out of the plaid shawl and reached them up around my neck, you were my own bairn. I had lost two little ones, just like Jeanie's mother lost her son. I needed you as much as you needed me. What an enchanting babe you were!"

The coldness inside me melted away like snow in the noon sun. The words "heart of my heart" sang over and over within me. I rested my head against Mother's shoulder as though I were Hugh's age and not nearly ten.

"Why didn't you tell me about Kirsty before?" I asked.

"Because of Hamish," Mother said, surprising herself as much as me. "He told you you were his sister and I was your mother. So we let it go. I planned to explain it all to you when you asked but you never did. Your father suggested we change your name to Gordon for simplicity's sake and, in his will, he asked us to adopt you legally. You were officially Elspet Mary Iveson until then, you know. We had always felt you were ours but the adoption made it clear to others as well. Do you remember your mother at all?"

I thought away back to my first misty memories but the arms I remembered holding me and rocking me were Mother's. I shook my head a little uncertainly. The bits I held onto were a song, a sprig of heart's-ease and a closeness too distant to be counted.

"It isn't surprising. You were just three," Mother said, stroking my fair hair gently. "I don't think Hamish remembers you aren't his real sister any longer. If he does, he never says."

I laughed aloud suddenly. I felt as light as thistledown. I felt like a soap bubble floating in a summer wind. I felt free and I felt safe at one and the same time.

"What's your scheme?" I asked dreamily.

"Wait and see," Mother said, setting me on my own two feet and going to mix today's cornbread. "It may not work."

"How long will I need to wait?" I pressed her.

"About an hour," she said. "Now get the broom and sweep this cabin floor. It'll help pass the time."

19

Mother's Scheme

While I swept, I waited, not at all certain what to expect. Then, at long last, I heard running footsteps.

Crash! The door of our cabin burst open. Mrs. Mackay stood there looking wild. Jeanie was right behind her. Her face was pale with fright in spite of the long walk. Her sunbonnet was dangling down her back and one of her braids was coming loose. Mrs. Mackay was nearly as red as a beet.

"Where is he?" she half-shouted at my mother. "Where's my baby?"

She saw Jamie then. He was on the floor, playing happily

with Mother's button box. Mrs. Mackay swooped down and snatched him into her arms.

"You dinna like my scheme then?" my mother said, smiling at her. "I thought perhaps you'd be pleased to have that ugly wee changeling taken off your hands."

"God forgive me for ever thinking such a wicked thing!" Mrs. Mackay said, sinking down on the settle and hugging Jamie till he yelped. "Mr. Mackay had told me he'd look for the family soon but I did not let myself think about that. Then Jeanie came in with your letter. I read what you wrote and I tried to imagine our lives without the imp and my heart came close to breaking. We ran most of the way. I didn't even stop to tell her what was wrong, poor child. I shouted to Bridget to wait for my husband and tell him I was coming here. I had the craziest notion that I'd get here only to find he'd vanished."

"I thought it might be that way," Mother said. "You see, I had a boy and girl who died of diphtheria not long before I was given Elspet to raise. Her coming to me was like a gift straight from God. I was afraid the bairn might be gone from you before you kenned how much you cared for him. That would have been a tragedy. Your husband and Jeanie need him, you know."

"I know it, woman, but you might have given me an attack of apoplexy, sending me that letter. Then what would you have said to my husband?" Mrs. Mackay asked and, to our amazement, the two of them began to laugh as though they were our age.

I did not stay to listen to them. I knew I was Mother's own girl. And I knew that nothing could change that. Now I wanted to play with Jeanie. We would have to be quick. Soon Mrs. Mackay would decide it was time to go home and cook her husband's dinner.

"Come on, Jeanie," I hissed.

Jeanie understood at once. She rose and the two of us slipped out of the room, making no more noise than a pair of mice.

Jeanie's eyes were still wide with wonder when we stood in the late afternoon sunshine outside the cabin. But my attention was caught by a basket which had been set down by the cabin door. Inside it, something fluttered and clucked in an anxious way.

"What's that?" I asked, dropping to my knees to peer into it.

"Oh, Father must be here too," Jeanie said, laughing. "He said this morning he was going to bring your mother over a hen and a young cockerel. We planned to eat him before you arrived through the bush. Father said that would be ungrateful since our rooster brought us such good neighbours. I wonder where your Bridget is. The two of them must have followed us, bringing the birds as a present. They must have figured out we were all right and gone to help out in the byre."

"That's where they are," I said. "I can hear Bridget singing. She always sings to the cow while she milks her."

Purrkin came prowling around the basket. His yellow eyes gleamed. His back arched. His tail bushed out to twice its normal size.

"No, Purrkin," I said, batting his nose away. "They aren't for your dinner either. Let's go and start Father making them a nice, safe coop."

"Your mother is … She's wonderful," Jeanie burst out, her face alight with joy as she finally understood what my mother's note had actually said. "Mam was beside herself when she read the letter. Do you think your mother would really have taken Jamie if Mam had stuck to not wanting him?"

I settled down on the broad step to think this over. But I found I did not have to think. I knew the answer as surely as I knew my own name was Elspet Mary Gordon.

"Of course she would," I told Jeanie. "But thank goodness she didn't have to. I think Jamie is bonny but three brothers are enough for any girl."

"I miss mine," Jeanie said, her voice husky. "Mam never notices but Father and I miss Alastair terribly."

I knew it was true. I still had a part of me, deep inside, that shrank from the very idea of loss. I reached out and picked a stalk of heart's-ease and held the soft pansy petals against my cheek and felt better.

"Maybe she'll notice now," I said slowly. "My mother lost two children before she had me. She'll help your mother somehow."

"She already has."

Then, inside the basket, the little rooster tried crowing. The whirring noise it made sounded so funny that both of us burst out laughing. I was still sitting next to the basket. I leaned over and spoke to him through its woven lid.

"Don't fret, little rooster. It's a new world but you're in the place where you belong. Jeanie and I didn't want to leave home but we did. And now, home is here."

Jeanie sat down next to me and looked dreamily at the golden September afternoon.

"Yes," she said so softly I could barely catch the words. "This is our new belonging place. We've all come home at last."

Acknowledgments

*T*his book would not have been written if it weren't for my ancestors who left their ain folk in the British Isles and so, without knowing us, made me and my siblings Canadians.

James Dow, a stonemason who came to Canada from Scotland as a child, built our present home in 1857 for his wife, Elspet, and the family they planned to have. I gave my heroine Elspet's first name as a way of thanking the Dows. I moved the building of the house back ten years to 1847 so that I could have Elspet born on my birthday one hundred years earlier. She writes her book in the "birthing room" which is now my study. In a sense, she herself was born in this room, since I first wrote of her here.

My thanks also go to many writers, both past and present, who provided me with a feeling for the time in which the Rosses and Gordons lived and who answered many of my dozens of questions. The two people to whom I owe the greatest debt are David Beattie and Barbara Greenwood. Dave's book about Nichol Township in pioneer days not only provided me with lots of background material but included the anecdote which gave me the urge to write. He told of one family realizing they had neighbours when they heard a rooster crowing and how they blazed a trail through the bush to find his owners. Barbara Greenwood told me such useful facts as what people wore, what they ate, how they worked and what their houses were like. She did this in her book *Pioneer Story* and by reading this manuscript and pointing out mistakes or unlikely happenings. Without the help of these people, my story could not have been written.

Others whom I consulted or read were Janet Lunn, who also read the manuscript at an early stage and assured me that it would make a book, and Marianne Brandeis, Claire Mackay, Bonnie Callen, the archivist at the Wellington County Museum, Helen Cunningham, Linda Bawden, Tim and Lydia Sullivan, Susanna Moodie and Catharine Parr Traill, Louisa May Alcott, Ben Wicks, Rosemary Sutcliff and Robert Burns.

The information which is historically correct came from the above. The incorrect bits are all my own. If you discover a glaring error, write and tell me and we may try to correct it in later editions.

I do know that Elspet's writing has a more modern sound than it would have done had she really written it in 1847, and her family's speech is not as broad Scots as it would have been, but I have done my best to get the flavour

right. I did want my readers to have no trouble compre-
hending what was being said. My mother, when she was
small, could not understand the broad Scots speech of her
own grandmother.

I had great fun helping Elspet get her story down. But it
is her story and I also want to thank her for taking over and
bringing fully alive a book which was initially written in the
third person. Once she got her hand on that pen Granny
Ross gave her, the book grew far more lively and I had a
much better time helping her to finish it.

3 1221 08469 5456